THRIVE

MARY BORSELLINO

CANCELLED

CLAN
DESTINE
PRESS

First published in Australia 2015
by Clan Destine Press

PO Box 121 Bittern
Victoria 3918 Australia

National Library of Australia Cataloguing-in-Publication entry

Author: Borsellino, Mary

Title: Thrive

ISBN   (pbk) 978-0-9942619-9-1

over Design: Motivating Marketing

Design & Typesetting: Clan Destine Press

Printed and bound in Australia: Lightning Source

www.clandestinepress.com.au

For Beth and Regan

1

Hannah, the girl in the red rabbit mask, brings food to Olivia's cell twice a day. Hannah is two or three years older than Olivia, but no taller and much thinner, and she stares at the trays of food – rice and gravy and vegetables – as if these small, cold meals are the most important thing she's ever seen and much, much more valuable than Olivia's money.

Two meals is less than Olivia's used to, but on the third day she pushes her hunger out of her mind as much as she can and eats only a small portion of the meal before offering the tray to Hannah.

'Do you want some?'

'I'm not supposed to,' Hannah says, but Olivia can see her eyes behind the red rabbit mask, and Hannah's eyes are more like those of a starving wolf than any kind of rabbit.

'Who am I gonna tell?' Olivia replies, gesturing to the tiny, empty cement space of the room. That makes Hannah smirk. It's the first smile Olivia's seen from her.

'Go on. Really.' Olivia holds the tray out again, and after another moment's hesitation Hannah takes it from her.

Hannah eats like she expects the food to be snatched away from her at any moment, scooping mouthfuls in, almost without stopping to chew. Her sleeve falls back as she raises the spoon to her mouth again, and Olivia can see that Hannah's skin looks sore and tight around the ports installed in her thin wrist. She must have had them put in very young for her body to have grown that much around them.

That makes Olivia feel sorry for her. That Hannah had ports

put in and yet wound up here, masked and starving, is the most unfair thing Olivia has ever seen in her life.

'Do you guys have my schoolbag?' she asks Hannah as Hannah eats, 'Or have you sent it to my parents as proof of life or whatever? I'm asking because my glasses are in there and I want to take my contact lenses out.'

'We have it. I'll ask,' Hannah says. She eats the next bite of food more slowly, like she's realised that Olivia gave it to her in exchange for glasses. Olivia's pretty sure that people who're kidnapped aren't supposed to make little unspoken trades like that, but she can't see why not. This whole stupid awful thing is supposed to be about giving everyone something they want, isn't it? The maskers want money, Olivia's parents want Olivia back. Everyone wins. Hannah wants dinner and Olivia wants her glasses.

Olivia also wants to know how much they think she's worth, but hasn't found a way to ask that won't sound weird and creepy.

'I'll see what I can do,' says Hannah.

Olivia smiles. 'Thank you.'

'Don't,' Hannah says sharply, putting down the spoon and leaving the room. Olivia notices that despite the dramatic exit, Hannah finished all the food before departing.

Olivia's room used to be a store room. It has little holes in a spaced-out, regular pattern around the walls where shelving used to be attached to them. Everything's been scrubbed, so it isn't dusty or dirty. Olivia appreciates that, and makes a note that she should tell Hannah to say thank you to the other captors on Olivia's behalf.

It sucks being locked in here, but Olivia's always cheered herself up by noticing all the ways things could suck even more than they do. Like: they gave her a bucket with a lid to use as a toilet, which is about a thousand times better than a bucket without a lid would have been. There's a flickering, faintly buzzing bare lightbulb attached to the ceiling, and the switch is located by the door so she can turn it on or off as she wants. There's a small, slatted window high up on one wall, which doesn't do much in the way of light but keeps her from running out of air to breathe, and that's absolutely something that belongs in the "plus" column of things going on in her life right now.

The bedroll they've given her doesn't stop the cement floor from being hard and cold, but she has a blanket and a pillow. At home she has quilts and cushions and everything else she could possibly want for a good night's sleep, but since Hannah doesn't even seem to get much food, Olivia suspects that comfortable bedding doesn't happen much in her kidnappers' lives. She's sure that they've given her the same level of luxury that they have themselves; maybe better.

It's not like she *likes* being held hostage; but it's not especially awful, considering.

A few hours later, Hannah comes back with Olivia's schoolbag in her hands.

'Am I allowed to say thank you now, or are you gonna get all weird and broody at me again if I do?' Olivia asks.

She can't tell for certain, what with the mask in the way, but she's sure that Hannah rolls her eyes.

'You're *weird*,' Hannah says.

'You're a *masker*,' Olivia retorts, dumping her school supplies on the floor and picking up the case of contacts stuff from the resulting pile of rubble.

'Yeah, but that's a cool kind of weird,' insists Hannah. Olivia snorts.

'Please. Anything that needs to be stridently defended as cool is automatically not cool. And *oooh*, scary, I got ambushed by a bunny and a cat and a fox and a mouse. What a joke.'

It's a lie, though, the bravado. Olivia's certain that Hannah isn't fooled for a second. Being grabbed like that had been terrifying, her face covered by a pillow case as she was thrown into the back of a van. Olivia hadn't known before that moment that it truly was possible to be so frightened that she couldn't even scream.

The memory makes her hands shake, so she puts aside the contacts case for the time being and looks up at Hannah instead.

Hannah's hands are a little lighter than Olivia's own. The rest of her skin is covered by her worn, faded clothes and her mask.

'Are the others your family? Your parents?' Olivia asks. Hannah shakes her head.

'No. My parents are dead.'

Olivia wants to say 'I'm sorry', but knows that to do so is risking another abrupt exit from Hannah, and Olivia doesn't want her to go.

'They're just a gang I'm running with,' Hannah goes on, breaking the short silence. 'I don't care one way or the other about them, and they don't care about me. It's a job, not a family. What's that?'

She points at a smaller drawstring bag among the stuff from inside Olivia's schoolbag. It's printed with a design of cutesy cartoon sharks and dolphins.

'Oh. My swimming stuff. I would've had gym today.' Her hands are steadier now, so Olivia starts taking out her contacts. 'I really love it. I'm shitty at it, but I still love it. I had to beg my parents to let me do it. My dad wanted me to do riding instead. I had to really fight for it.'

'You must love it,' Hannah agrees, a dubious note in her voice, as though she can't imagine why anyone would.

Olivia's glasses feel comforting on her nose, like there's a thin layer of force-field between her and everything around her. Usually she only wears her glasses at home, in the evenings. Her mother says she's prettier when people can see her face properly, so in public she always wears her contacts. It would be silly to worry about being pretty among maskers, though. They don't think a person's face has anything at all to do with who they are.

'I swam in the real ocean once.'

'Bull,' Hannah says bluntly. 'I don't care how rich you are, nobody swims in the ocean. All the money in the world isn't gonna stop you from rotting inside and out if you get that shit on you.'

'Not *this* ocean, loser,' Olivia shoots back, unsurprised by

Hannah's protest. 'One of the safe ones. You can stay in the water for an hour and not get sick at all. The hotel that owned the area even had sand imported and heaped up all along the edge of the water, so it was like being on a beach from an old movie. There was a palm tree.'

'If they'd gone to that much trouble to simulate it, why not have a tide pool like everywhere else, where people could stay in it as long as they liked?'

'Because the real ocean is nothing like a tide pool. Nothing.'

'Well excuse me, your majesty. Us ordinary mortals don't have your wisdom on such matters.'

'One day I hope you *do* see the ocean. I hope you get to swim in it. I hope I'm there to call you dumb names when it happens.'

Hannah shakes her head. 'How much money do you *have*, that you can do insane, impossible, fairy-tale things like swim in the ocean?'

'Not me. My dad. I don't even get pocket money – I have to ask him to buy anything I want. My mother has to do that as well. Since our servants buy the groceries, he says she'd just spend it on stupid stuff. He gets to pick what dresses she wears. That's where his money comes from, dresses. He has a factory.'

'*Dresses*? Nobody gets rich enough for a proper kidnapping from *dresses*.' The look Hannah gives Olivia is dripping in disbelief, even with the mask in the way.

'Well, it's not *only* dresses. Shirts and blouses and socks and things, too. All the cotton and wool that they use is unmodded, so people pay a lot for it.'

Hannah gives a low whistle. 'I bet. That's crazy.'

'Unmodded sheep have this oil in their wool, lanolin. I'm allergic to it. My dad still makes me wear clothes made in his factory, even when they itch me. He says it'd be bad for his reputation if his own family were ever seen dressed in anything but his label.'

'What's so special about unmodded that makes it so expensive?'

9

Olivia shrugs, as puzzled as Hannah. 'My dad says it's more *authentic* than other kinds. Here, this is one of the most expensive ones he sells.' She picks up her coat from where it lies crumpled among her school stuff and passes it to Hannah.

'It's so soft,' Hannah marvels, stroking her hand over the sheepskin as if it's the pelt of a small warm animal.

'Astrakhan. That's what this kind's called. It's not wool, really. It's still on the hide,' Olivia explains, surprised at how much of her father's lectures she's retained. 'I guess it's leather, or fur. Skin. The ewes are cut open while they're pregnant and the foetus is skinned. That's how you get astrakhan.'

Hannah pulls her hand away from the coat as abruptly as someone touching flame. Her face wears an expression of deep revulsion for a few seconds, but it fades soon enough. Olivia thinks it must be hard to hold onto horror for very long if you live in Hannah's world. Otherwise you'd never have a chance to feel anything else.

'Gross,' is all Hannah says, handing the coat back.

2

The next morning, Olivia has a runny nose. She's achy and tired all over and is plain old *cranky*. She wants a cup of chicken soup and her own bed and cartoons to watch.

'Has my dad given you money yet?' she snaps when Hannah brings her the early meal of the day, though she knows the answer must be "no" or she wouldn't still be here.

'He says he wants to negotiate with us, but every time we try to actually talk seriously with him, it's like he's stalling,' Hannah answers, obviously seeing no reason to tell Olivia anything but the truth.

'He probably hopes you'll get sick of me and settle for much cheaper,' Olivia quips, only half-joking.

'Your father's an asshole.'

Nobody's actually said that out loud to Olivia before. She blinks. 'Yeah, I guess so. Joke's on him though, huh? Kidnappers kill hostages if the families don't pay.'

Hannah snorts. 'He probably thinks we wouldn't dare.'

Something hard and icy in her tone makes Olivia shudder. All at once she's reminded that, whatever weird rapport they've formed, Hannah is part of the masker gang that holds Olivia's life in their hands.

'Hey, no,' Hannah says, putting down the tray of food and grabbing Olivia's hand between her own. 'Nobody's killing anyone, 'k? If he's still being a wad in another couple of days, we'll cut your hair off and send it to him. He'll pay right away when that happens, trust me. They always want to stop it before it gets to an ear or finger.'

Hair. That's fine. Olivia doesn't care about her hair.

'Have you done this lots of times before, then?' she asks.

Hannah nods. 'Yeah, lots. Well... not me, exactly. No. I haven't. I only threw in with this crew a few months ago, but they've done it a lot. That's why I wanted in with them, because they get shit done, they don't just sit around talking and talking and starving down to bones, like the last lot I was with.'

Olivia decides not to point out that all she and Hannah have done since Olivia got here is talk and talk. Instead she asks, 'Were you a red rabbit with them, too?'

'Yep. That's me, always. One and only,' Hannah says, flicking a fingertip against one of the worn leather ears.

'I can't imagine you without it,' confesses Olivia.

'You probably won't ever see my face any other way. I mean, unless I die while you get rescued,' Hannah says. 'You might see my underneath-face then. Anyway, enough talk. Eat your breakfast and you'll feel better.'

'Cut my hair off now. Tell the others that I don't care. Do it now, prove to my parents that you're serious.'

'And you call *me* melodramatic,' teases Hannah. Then, in a less playful tone, she adds, 'I'll tell the others, okay? We're all getting antsy. They might go for it.'

Olivia doesn't see Hannah again until after nightfall, when the room's getting cold enough to make her shiver. There's a camera, a newspaper front page, and a slightly rusty pair of shears in Hannah's hands.

'Oooh, my first fashion shoot,' Olivia says, determined to be light-hearted about this. It's going to happen no matter what; the only variable she has any control over is how she reacts to it. She's going to be as optimistic as possible.

Hannah cuts Olivia's hair off quickly, taking the ponytail in one snip and then clipping away the rest.

'My head's gonna get cold,' Olivia grumbles, trying not to look at the ponytail on the ground beside her, the long, thick locks that her mother said were her best feature.

'Drape your blanket over it,' suggests Hannah.

'I'll look like a dork if I do that.'

'Nobody's gonna see you except me, and I know you *are* a dork. Hold this.' Hannah shoves the newspaper page into Olivia's hands and steps back, snapping a few shots with the camera. The flash makes lights dance in Olivia's vision. 'Proof that we did it today, you see?'

'Yeah, yeah, I got it,' Olivia nods. Her head feels so light without her hair. It's weird.

That night it takes her a long time to get to sleep. She tells herself it's because of the cold, because of trying to huddle up small enough under the blanket that she can cover her head as well.

That doesn't explain why she's crying, though.

She doesn't miss her parents. Not like she's supposed to; not as much as someone in her position should. She feels guilty that the girl they'll get back at the end of all this is going to be even more disappointing than she already was, even uglier and stranger.

It's nearly dawn before she manages to drift off, exhausted from her tears.

3

'Your reader's full of shit,' Hannah announces instead of saying hello the next morning. Olivia didn't notice that it was missing from her stuff. Hannah's waving the thin slate in one hand. 'There's nothing on here but schoolbooks and assigned novels. *Nothing.*'

'So?'

'Ugh.' Hannah shakes her head in despair. 'You don't even know how great books are, do you? You're as empty and full of shit as your reader.'

'Hey, fuck you too,' Olivia scowls. 'What am I *supposed* to have on my reader, then? A reader that the government can look through *any time they feel like it*, might I add. Sure, I'll fill that up with illegal shit right now, what a great idea!'

'Lame. There's some okay stuff on the permit list, if you bother to look, which I bet you never have. And jailbreaking readers so they can't be scanned by wifi is kid's stuff, come on. I had to hack part of it before I even turned it on so the GPS wouldn't kick in.'

'Don't jailbreak my reader, asshole! People get in trouble for that.'

'*People get in trouble for that,*' Hannah mimics in a sarcastic baby-talk voice.

'Cut it out. Just because I don't care about your dumb books doesn't mean you get to be a humourless asshole. Even straight mathematics is about a thousand percent less stupid than reading.'

'I can see your natural aptitude for it, with terms like 'a

14

thousand percent',' snarks Hannah. Olivia rolls her eyes. 'You've been locked up your whole life,' Hannah goes on, 'In a cell so much tinier than this room right here. You don't know... you haven't got any idea how great words and stories can be.'

'And *you* don't know how beautiful numbers are. Patterns, puzzles, interconnected systems. The whole universe is made of that stuff!'

'Whatever, you stubborn lunatic.' Hannah's voice is breezy. 'I'm gonna bring you some of my paperbacks, and give you pop quizzes on them in exchange for your meals. If you don't read them, you don't eat.'

Olivia splutters in futile outrage. 'You can't give me *homework*! You're my *kidnapper*!'

'I'm pretty sure that means I get to do what I want,' comes the retort. Sure enough, when Olivia next sees Hannah, the rabbit-masked girl is carrying a pile of battered books with softened corners.

She puts them down beside Olivia and gives the uppermost cover a fond pat. 'There. Pick whichever you like; I've read them all often enough to think up quiz questions on the fly. Just let me know which one you've read when I come in later.'

Olivia can't imagine being thrilled about reading a book once, let alone liking the experience enough to do it multiple times. She's got no real say in the matter, though, so she picks up the top book – *The Day of the Triffids* by John Wyndham – and opens it to the first page.

4

For the rest of her life, no matter how often she's read it or where she is at the time, *The Day of the Triffids* always takes her back to that little cement room, to the changing shape of the square of light on the floor as the sun moves across the sky outside the window.

The fear and boredom of her own captive life falls away as she follows Josella and Bill on their desperate escape from apocalyptic London, out into the countryside. She's afraid when they are, she cries when they cry, she hears the plaintive notes of a song across the darkened ruins right along with them.

When it seems for a while that maybe they can build a new life on the farm they've filled with other misfits they've found along the way, protect its perimeter from danger and be happy, Olivia's heart sings for them.

When, at the very end, they have to run away again because the greedy tyrants they've fled in London have found them once more, Olivia's heart is so full of so many different things that it's going to explode for sure.

As soon as Hannah opens the door that night, Olivia's on her feet, meeting Hannah and taking the tray from her excitedly.

'I read *Day of the Triffids*. It was *amazing*.'

'Am I allowed to say "I told you so"?' Hannah asks, following her deeper into the room. 'Because I did.'

'You didn't *tell* me anything. You threatened to withhold my food,' Olivia corrects her without malice. It's hard to be angry at Hannah for giving Olivia something so precious. She sits and begins to eat.

'Semantics.' Hannah brushes away the accusation with a wave. 'If you liked that, I think I put my copy of *The Midw–*'

Bang!

The end of her sentence is drowned out by a nearby door being kicked open; and then, much louder – so shatteringly loud that Olivia can feel it in every tooth and bone in her body – the sound of a gunshot.

She's on her feet before her brain has registered that she's going to move. Hannah's frozen on the spot but remembers how to move at the same moment Olivia does. They draw closer to one another by instinct, their movements matched as they both start in fright at the noise of a second gunshot rapidly followed by a third.

There are seconds – less than seconds – of time, but it's enough for Olivia to act. She grabs one of the long ears of Hannah's red rabbit mask and pulls up, wrenching the whole thing away from the other girl's face in one sharp motion that sends it flying into the corner of the room, among the pile of stuff from Olivia's schoolbag.

Hannah's hair is cropped short; not as short as Olivia's own hacked-off locks but nearly so. She's younger than Olivia had guessed. They might be the same age. Hannah looks even more frightened than Olivia feels.

Olivia grabs Hannah in a hug and clings on, pressing Hannah's face down against her own shoulder as the door bangs open.

The guy standing there is so broad and tall that he fills the whole space of the doorframe, barring any chance of freedom as effectively as the door had.

'She was here when I got here,' Olivia says, clinging tight to Hannah, praying that Hannah will go along with this flimsy excuse for a plan. 'She doesn't speak. I don't know how long she's been a hostage here.'

The gun in his hands is huge. Horrifying. Olivia knows with a sick rush of cold through her limbs that she'll see that gun in her nightmares for the rest of her life.

17

He gives Hannah the barest of glances, his concentration on Olivia. 'Your father sent us,' he tells her. 'Come on.'

They follow him out the door, Hannah clutching as tightly to Olivia's hand as Olivia is to hers. Two dirty, frightened girls, led together through the remains of a masker hideout.

In the main room, the other three kidnappers are lying where they fell. One, the fox, has a bullet hole through the forehead of his mask, and the blood looks almost fake, too red, where it's pooled under him. The mouse and the cat were trying to get away when they died and so their wounds are on their backs, their bodies face-down on the concrete floor.

Hannah chokes on a sob. Olivia squeezes her hand tighter.

Two other men, broad and tall as the first, are checking each room with their guns at the ready. As she follows the first man through the space, towards the entrance, Olivia clears her throat and addresses all three of them.

'That's all. It was only three: mouse, cat, and fox.' She hopes it'll be a long, long time before anyone discovers that there was a red rabbit as well.

It doesn't surprise her when they all ignore her.

Outside, the air is colder than it was in the building but there are no smells of gunpowder, shit or blood, so Olivia takes a deep breath despite the chill.

'Here.' The man points to a van. The symmetry of her arrival to this place and her departure strikes Olivia as weirdly funny. She wants to laugh out loud, or maybe cry.

Olivia climbs in, pulling Hannah after her before anyone can say otherwise. It would be much too dangerous for Hannah to run now; perhaps an opportune moment will present itself later.

The man climbs into the driver's seat.

'What about the others?' Olivia asks. There are tears on Hannah's face now, and her hand is trembling hard in Olivia's grasp. Strangely, Olivia's own fear has melted away. Every nerve in her body is thrumming, so much so that she's lightheaded, but she isn't scared. Saving Hannah is all that matters for now. There'll be time to feel scared later.

'They'll meet me later, after they've checked for others,' the man tells her. Olivia holds back from telling him again that there were only three.

Instead, she asks, 'Are we going straight to my home, or to a hospital first?'

'Hospital. It's regulation.'

Inside she almost wilts with relief, but outside all she does is nod and squeeze Hannah's hand.

'What's your name, hon?' the man asks Hannah now, looking at them both in his rear-view mirror. Hannah shakes her head, gulping on her sobs.

'We can ask the police if they recognise her when we're at the hospital,' Olivia says. She's sure Hannah can get away before that happens, and even if they get a picture of her then, well, she's a masker, right? Hopefully that means they don't have any pictures of her real face on file as connected to any crimes.

The man's telephone rings, the shrill beeps making both girls start in surprise. The streetlights are painting moving stripes of light over them as they drive past each one.

The man says 'mm', 'mhm' and 'yeah' a few times, then hangs up. He meets Olivia's eyes in the mirror again before addressing her.

'That was your dad. The hospital we were meeting at just got locked down with some infection thing. Your parents got the staff to let them out of the ER, but we can't meet them there now, obviously. We're going to St Bridget's over the hill instead. It's about 45 minutes away, so try to get some sleep if you want.'

'There aren't any closer hospitals?' Olivia asks. She's not very surprised that her dad didn't ask to talk to her, even after she'd been kidnapped and then violently rescued. His brain doesn't work like that.

'None worth going to,' the man answers her.

Forty-five minutes is a long time to sit in silent fear, but

Olivia's almost used to it after so long spent in the room. She's learned how to retreat into her head, where time doesn't matter in the same way. As skills go, she thinks it's probably more creepy than useful, but it does mean that right now she's not as likely to throw up from fear as she might've done before everything started.

Instead, she spends the time trying to come up with a way for Hannah to get away, but Olivia's life experiences offer no toehold from which to mount a daring criminal escape.

After about twenty minutes, Hannah stirs, sitting up straighter. Her voice, when she speaks, is a rasping whisper.

'May I use your phone?' she asks the man.

He passes it into the back seat. Hannah enters a number with unsteady hands and then brings the phone to her ear. Olivia can't hear a dial tone or the purr of ringing, but after a few seconds, Hannah speaks rapidly.

'Hi Annie. It's Lissa. I know, sweetheart, I know. I've missed you so much too, my little red riding hood. Can you put Mama on?'

Hannah's voice is croaky and quiet, and after exactly three quick, shallow breaths of silence she speaks again. 'Mama. Mama, it's Lissa. I'm on my way to St Bridget's. I'm safe. Please come get me. I've missed you so much.'

Without waiting for any reply, she ends the call and passes the phone back through between the front seats.

'My mother will collect me,' she whispers to the man. Olivia does her best to hide her confusion and surprise, because she thinks Hannah said she didn't have parents. This must be someone else she knows, someone willing to help with an alibi at a moment's notice. Olivia wonders what Hannah has promised in exchange for the favour, or if the mystery person already owed Hannah for something in the past.

'She'll give you money,' Hannah goes on. 'Not so much as the ransom was. She doesn't have that. But some.' Her inflections and manner are totally different to those of the Hannah that Olivia's started to know, but that doesn't mean much of anything.

It's not like Olivia has any idea about Hannah's life or where she'll go or what she'll do now. And there's never going to be a chance to ask.

'You don't have to pay me, sweetheart,' the man tells Hannah. 'We've already been compensated for our trouble. You were in the right place at the right time. It's your lucky day.'

'She'll still pay you,' Hannah insists. Olivia squeezes her hand again, hoping it'll convey to Hannah how smart Olivia thinks her words are. Giving the men some money will make them like her, give them a reason not to question anything she or her "mother" tell them.

It seems to Olivia that this whole emergency plan is going to leave Hannah deeply indebted to whoever is coming to her rescue, but that can't be helped. Better to be indebted and alive than cold and bloodied on a cement floor like the others.

Olivia wonders if they, like Hannah, were younger than she guessed. Mouse, cat, fox. Maybe they were the same age as her.

5

Finally, finally, they reach St Bridget's, and Olivia and Hannah climb out of the van still clasping each other's hands. Then there's a flurry of people all around them, and raised voices, and Olivia's parents are grabbing her tightly in frantic hugs, and a woman is calling Hannah "Lissa" and catching her up as well. Olivia and Hannah's hands get pulled apart from one another in the confusion and Olivia doesn't see her again after that.

She gets bundled up and whisked away to a private room, where her mother cries and her father looks relieved and they both fuss over her as she tries to assure them that she's fine, she's fine.

The doctors check her for concussion and bruises and broken bones and malnutrition, and put her on an IV that makes her so cold that her teeth chatter. Then she's allowed to take a long, warm shower that is absolute heaven against her aches and pains.

When she's dressed in fluffy new pyjamas and given hot cocoa and told that she needs to be kept overnight for observation, Olivia is so overwhelmed with people being kind and nice and gentle that she starts to cry, which makes everyone even kinder and nicer and more gentle.

'Is the other girl still here? Lissa?' Olivia asks a nurse. He shakes his head.

'No. She and her mother left after they were reunited. This is a very exclusive hospital.' He pats her on the arm. 'I'm sure she's fine.'

So that's that.

6

After that there's nothing to do but wait for the other shoe to drop. Olivia wakes up, night after night, frozen in terror and drenched in her own clammy sweat. She's never needed a lot of sleep, but even so it's not long before her parents notice the shadows under her eyes and the way she jumps in frightened surprise whenever anyone speaks to her.

They think it's post-traumatic stress. Olivia feels like the worst kind of jackass, because she wishes they were right. She knows post-traumatic stress is a big awful gross thing that ruins the lives of the people who have it, but it seems so much cleaner and simpler than this secret she's carrying. Trauma would be hers to work through and overcome, but the question of whether she'll be caught out as aiding and abetting a masker – the wilful facilitation of a crime – is not in her control. It'll happen, or it won't. All Olivia can do is wait.

After a while the waiting, the terror, fades and shifts and settles in for the long-term. The worry doesn't go away. It insinuates itself into the normal routine of emotions that Olivia has every day, like being bored or tired or lonely. She's always waiting, until she hardly notices the wait at all.

The main thing that's left of her initial fear is a sense of things being unfinished between her and Hannah. Olivia can't forget her, can't put the whole experience into the past. It doesn't feel over yet, and if nobody ever finds out what Olivia did, it never will be.

For all that her parents talk about the importance of closure, Olivia doesn't mind the thought that things will never be properly

23

finished between her and Hannah. It feels like there's still some connection between them, a part of each other they'll carry into their separate futures.

As time goes on, it's easier to talk about things. Eventually, Olivia is brave enough to raise the topic with her mother.

'Those security guys, the ones that rescued me… they were really good at their jobs.'

'Yes, darling, your father hired the best in the business. We wanted to be as sure as sure can be that we'd get you back safe and sound.'

'But...' Olivia frowns. 'If they were as expensive as all that, why not just pay the ransom and get me back that way?'

'That's not how things are done,' her mother answers stiffly. 'You know that.'

Knowing and understanding are different things, but Olivia thinks that saying so would cause trouble. Arguing with her parents never does any good.

'You missed your birthday while you were away,' her mother says, like Olivia's been at school camp or on holiday. 'We should have a party.'

'I don't have any hair,' Olivia reminds her. Olivia doesn't care about that, but she knows her mother does.

'We can buy you a good wig. Real hair,' her mother assures her.

'I don't want a wig.'

'Don't be difficult, sweetheart.' The words have a scolding edge, but then her mother's expression softens. 'Oh, my little darling,' she says, hugging Olivia close. 'Better to lose your hair than an earlobe or a finger, at least.'

Olivia misses Hannah.

7

Her parents send her to a new school, one with stronger security. Olivia thinks this is pointless; she's already been kidnapped. The extra protection is too late.

The kids at this new school are the kind of kids that Olivia's parents wish she was. They're perfectly groomed and work with quiet diligence and are horribly, horribly cruel to her and the others among them who don't fit in. They make up nicknames for the misfits, and mock their bodies and voices and families.

One of them trips Olivia as she's going down a flight of stairs one day, and she injures her elbows and chin so badly that she needs three stitches. The blood all over her school uniform makes her think of gunfire, and she idles over thoughts of the private security thugs bursting into the classroom and killing the bullies who torment her.

She doesn't think she'd be all that upset to see them die. She hadn't cried when it happened before, and the maskers had never been horrible to her like these kids are.

Olivia daydreams of violence, but her night dreams are softer and sadder. That's why she finally works up the courage to look for interesting books; she thinks giving her imagination more things to do during the day will make it quieter at night, and let her sleep better.

She has to buy a new reader. Her old one was left behind in the cement room, along with all her other schoolbag things.

Hannah was right about there being stuff worth reading in the legal archives. They contain lots of classic novels that someone decided must be harmless simply because they're old.

As if history were full of only safe and friendly thoughts and deeds.

Olivia's careful to space the interesting books out between drier texts, to hide her tracks on the system. Even reading the boring books is better than having nothing to do, and her dreams lose the worst of their dark edges.

Among the sanctioned fairy tales on the school server is a collection of ones that never got properly sanitised for modern readers. These stories are old and wild, full of blood and forests and fur and teeth and magic. Olivia wishes she could read them in privacy. She lives with a constant and pervading anxiousness at the thought that someone, somewhere, is paying attention to what she's accessing on her reader.

One of the stories in the collection is called *Donkeyskin*. It's a distant relation of *Cinderella*, Olivia thinks. The two have a common ancestor but they grew in very different directions. *Donkeyskin* is Olivia's favourite; it's one of the most important and strange things she's ever encountered.

If someone notices that a story like that is available, and that she reads it so much, something terrible might happen. Because *Donkeyskin* is the story of a little girl, a princess who grows up into a beautiful teenager, so beautiful that her own father – the King – decides he must marry her no matter what. Since Olivia's own father is so rich and respected, there are lots of people who'd like nothing better than to destroy him. If one of them is watching her reader in the data cloud, and notices how often she reads and re-reads *Donkeyskin*, it would only take one news article full of speculation and innuendo to ruin her father's hard-built reputation as a good and honest man.

While Olivia might not get on well with her father, she really does love him. More importantly, he has never done anything like the King in the story. Her father would kill anyone who tried to hurt his child.

That's not even a figure of speech; it's simple fact. The gunshots in her nightmares bear testament to that.

The King has nothing to do with why Olivia's captivated by

the story. It's how the girl escapes that enchants her. The princess stitches a disguise for herself out of fur and feathers and animal hides, helped by all the woodland creatures she's fed at her windowsill since she was small. They repay her kindness by giving little pieces of themselves, building her a costume as feral and strange as anything in the forest.

The princess leaves behind her home and her father and her name, and because the cloak she's sewn has tall, odd ears sticking up from the top, she calls herself Donkeyskin.

Donkeyskin carries three dresses from her princess life in her satchel, in case she ever needs to sell the jewels on them to buy food. She doesn't have anything to worry about, though. No sooner has she made her way to the next kingdom than she finds work as a scullery maid in the castle kitchens.

Nobody's kind to Donkeyskin. They kick over her bucket as she scrubs the floors because they didn't notice her there. She has to live off scraps from the kitchen plates because nobody remembers to save food for her. Nobody's kind, but nobody's nasty either. They just hardly see her, even in plain sight. The ugliness of her Donkeyskin disguise makes her invisible.

It makes Olivia think about the information updates everyone gets sent all the time, about how you're not allowed to wear this or that geometric makeup design on your face because it scrambles the facial recognition software in public cameras. Some hairstyles are illegal for the same reason, and of course there are maskers.

Olivia thinks Donkeyskin's way is smarter than any of those. Donkeyskin knew that the way to hide wasn't to do anything except to be ugly, to be too gross for anyone to want to pay attention. Not weird enough to be memorable, not strange enough to be noticed by anybody: just a part of the general noisy, crowded background of the world.

The story has a typical ending, of course. It's related to *Cinderella* after all. There are three royal balls and the princess puts aside her Donkeyskin costume and wears her three dresses, and the prince falls in love with her. She leaves behind a shoe at

27

the third ball by mistake when she runs away (because she has to run away; staying anywhere for too long without her disguise is too hard for her) and then the prince demands that every woman in the land try on the lost shoe to see if it fits. And Donkeyskin – who has fallen in love with the prince; she didn't mean to but she couldn't help it – goes along, and everyone scoffs and laughs that the weird ugly scullery maid wants to try, and the shoe fits and the prince loves her the same in rags or in ballgowns, and everyone is happy forever et cetera, et cetera.

Olivia doesn't care about that part. She's most interested in the beginning, when Donkeyskin runs away and starts anew. It's the best and bravest thing Olivia can imagine.

She tries to get braver in her own life. Feeling brave would be feeling something.

8

People in her class at school say that Sam, the boy who works at the souvlaki shop near the train station, is a grey market dealer. He can get just about anything: drugs, passwords, swipecards, signal-blocking fabric. So long as you've got enough money to pay him, he can set you up.

Olivia thinks she should feel afraid, or at least nervous, at the prospect of doing something so blatantly illegal. But she isn't. She doesn't feel much of anything. She hasn't since she was rescued.

The only times she's felt real since that night have been when she's lost in words, and none of the books she can get on her reader make her feel real enough. They're too nice, too safe. They don't have any challenge in them.

Olivia wants a book that makes her feel the way that Hannah's smirks did, dangerous and dared and ready for the adventure coming. A promise and a threat all at once.

Before the kidnapping, it was no big deal to tell her parents that she was going out after school and then get the train home, instead of getting picked up by a driver as she always is these days. Now her parents are super-paranoid about everything. It isn't like it's one of the scary train lines where bad stuff happens, or she's planning to be out late.

The best plan she can think of to stop them from worrying is to make up a half-truth. She tells them that she won't need the driver that afternoon; the school provides transport for kids in after-school clubs to get home from campus. This is all true, and if she doesn't actually tell them that she isn't in a club and has no plans to join one, well, it's not her fault that they interpreted her general statement of fact to be specifics about her afternoon, is it?

Olivia doesn't feel guilty for the lie. She doesn't think she'd feel guilty for it even if she were feeling things properly.

To give the lie a faint patina of truth, she hangs around the school for a while after classes end before heading towards the café where this Sam guy works.

The neighbourhoods around her school and her home are all nice ones, of course. They're clean and expensive and almost completely rebuilt. Her house is in an estate, where there isn't much garden between the houses but all of the houses are big and tall. Her school's in a more urban area, the grounds a blot of green among the endless stretch of high-rises.

To be honest, Olivia's looking forward to her train ride home almost as much as she's looking forward to buying a book. The route the tracks take, between the station near the souvlaki place and the station near her house, goes through one of the last pockets of ruin in the area. Block after block of flattened rubble, nothing but empty space and broken streetlights.

She heard her father talking about it once, about how the permits are in place and that building will start soon. She wants to see the empty space at least once before it's gone.

But that'll come later. First, she steps into the little café, and looks for the person who can give her words.

Sam is small and slightly-built, not as tall as her (though that's not uncommon; she's the tallest kid in her class at school and Sam doesn't seem to be any older than her and her schoolmates). His features remind her of the marble statues that decorate the outskirts of her parents' ballroom. Not only because his face is even-set and beautiful, but because there is something remote and still about him. She wonders if the lushness of his lip would yield to the touch of her fingertips, or if his olive skin would be smooth and implacable as stone.

A leather band is on his right wrist, black and unadorned, the kind that people wear when they want to hide ports.

'Can you get books?' she asks as soon as they're done exchanging names.

'Of course,' he answers straight away, his tone flat and matter-of-fact. If someone at school talked to her like that, she'd think they were being kind of rude and sort of an asshole, but she can see that Sam's twisting his hand and wrist at his side as he's talking to her. Olivia's pretty sure that when people fidget like that it means that they're nervous, so she isn't annoyed at him.

'Sorry, I phrased that stupidly,' she concedes. 'Can I buy a book, please?'

He nods and disappears into the kitchen area out the back of the café.

At a loss – is she meant to wait for him; should she follow – Olivia sits on the edge of a booth seat and looks around. Everything is brightly coloured and cheerful-looking, but worn down, like it's been a long time since anything was replaced or refreshed. She wonders how easy or difficult it is, working here instead of going to school.

One of the girls from her school, from an older grade than Olivia's, steps into the café and joins some out-of-uniform kids in the next booth over from where Olivia sits.

'The station's all closed down,' the girl tells her friends. 'Some loser jumped in front of the train and made a huge gory mess. It's gonna be hours before stuff's cleaned up and moving again.'

'Ugh, what a drag,' one of her friends answers.

Olivia feels faintly ill. It's not the death, exactly – her much more immediate brush with dead bodies is still a recent memory, after all. It's the idea of somebody being so close by to so many other people and nobody knowing that this person wanted to die, thought being dead was better than being alive. That the train driver would always remember that horrible, hideous second when they realised what was happening.

It makes her want to cry. It's the first real feeing she's had in months, and it's a lousy one.

Sam comes back into view, approaching her and handing

31

her a small paper bag. She shoves it into her schoolbag and gets out her wallet, handing him the money.

'Thanks,' she says.

'Your hands are shaking, and you're pale,' he notes.

'Yeah, uh, turns out that the train station's shut down,' she tells him. 'I'm gonna have to walk home. My parents are going to murder me if they find out.'

'My shift ends soon. If you wait, I can walk you home.'

Olivia wants to tell him that he doesn't have to, that it's fine, she'll be fine, but she's actually very grateful that he offered and so just nods. 'Okay. Thanks.'

Sam nods and goes behind the counter to serve the customers.

The package in her schoolbag is more exciting than any birthday-morning gift has ever been. The anticipation of opening it makes her giddy. Olivia can't help but think wryly that this is probably how girls her age are supposed to feel about crushes, rather than about secret books.

'All right, we can go now,' Sam says, walking to the door without waiting for her to gather her things and follow.

The air's sharp outside, one of the bad briny winds that promises water contamination with the next rain. Olivia wonders if the souvlaki café puts its prices up when that happens. The canteen at her school puts a 20% levy on everything to make up for the higher cost of the water, but Olivia doesn't know if people who buy food from the café can pay that much extra, even for a week or two.

Maybe she could offer to calculate some different price plans for them, to find a balance between charging enough without charging too much. Sam might think that's weird for her to suggest, though.

'I give this list to my new customers,' Sam tells her, handing over a folded slip of paper as they walk side-by-side down the darkening footpath. 'It's fifty books you won't have heard of, but that are sanctioned for download. In case you need something new to read before you make it back to me.'

'That's not good business practice on your part, is it?' Olivia asks, tucking the list into the pocket of her coat. 'Giving people things to read that they don't pay you for?'

Sam shrugs. 'I've never aspired to be an economist.'

'I have,' admits Olivia. 'I had a whole reader full of economy books. They were the only kind I liked to read, until…' She trails off. Until she'd lost the reader in a little cement room. Until a girl in a red rabbit mask had dumped a stack of paperbacks on the floor next to her and demanded she choose one.

'Thank you,' she says, instead of finishing her sentence. 'I'll check it out.'

'You like it out here,' Sam remarks, looking at her and then around them. 'Even though it's ruins. Your posture is more confident. You look happier. You're not a town mouse. You like it better in the open.'

Olivia remembers that story from when she was young. The town mouse and the country mouse are friends, but each hates everything about where the other lives. They try to compromise for the sake of affection, but neither is really happy visiting the other. She always thought it was a sad story.

'What about you?' she asks Sam. 'Are you a town mouse or a country mouse?'

He scuffs at the ground with his foot. 'Neither, really. I'm a robot mouse.'

9

She opens the paper bag in her bedroom that night, when there's not much chance of anyone disturbing her and seeing what she's doing. Her pulse is a nervous flutter as she takes the ancient, half-collapsed paperback out of its wrapping.

Dark Carnival by Ray Bradbury. The cover is lurid, black and red, grey photos picked out in halftone dots and collaged with no sense or order.

Olivia begins to read and doesn't stop until her alarm clock goes off at 6:30am the next morning. She hides the book on the top shelf of her closet, behind her rarely-worn, most expensive formal clothes.

The stories in the book are little slivers cut with a sharp and gleaming knife – vampire families having happy reunions, scythes reaping fields of souls. Nightmares pinned down with ink, seeping blackly into Olivia's spongy brain and clattering heart.

The one she returns to time and time again, that haunts her through her days, is called *The Small Assassin*. It's about a mother who thinks her baby's trying to kill her. It cries at night to stop her from getting any rest, so she'll end up sick and tired and catch pneumonia.

When the mother falls down the stairs and dies, her doctor decides she was right all along, and the story ends with the doctor getting his scalpel out of his bag. Getting ready to kill the baby.

The story lingers like a taste in the back of Olivia's throat, like grit in her eye. She thinks it might be the saddest story in the world. The baby didn't ask to be born bad. Nobody can help it, being born however they're born. If a mother won't love it and a doctor won't care for it, what's left? Who takes care of the babies that are born wicked, the stepsisters and queens and black knights of fairy stories, the small murderers of horror fiction? Who makes sure they're fed and warm and safe?

Even the ones born strange need someone who loves them, don't they?

Sometimes she is very, very lonely.

Her mother is disappointed that she doesn't wear her contacts anymore. 'Your glasses make you look so plain. Ordinary.'

Her mother talks of disappointments and her father doesn't talk at all, preferring to punish her with silence and lack of attention. Olivia's always grateful to leave for school in the mornings, and lingers away from home as long as she can in the afternoons. At least at school she doesn't have to feel guilty about resenting the teachers that dislike her. When biting rage wells up against her father and mother, it always makes her feel she's failed at something important.

Sometimes her father doesn't speak to her for weeks on end, and then without warning he'll tell her all about his day over the dinner table. He makes it clear through this renewed attention that she has been forgiven for the C in History or the messy handwriting or the torn stockings at an important child's birthday party.

Olivia is so tired of being forgiven.

10

After school the next day, she goes to the souvlaki place and walks through to the kitchen at the back. One thing she's learned from knowing people like her father is that if you appear to know where you're going and why you belong there, nobody will stop you or ask questions.

Sam's refilling the salt shakers from a larger container. He looks up as she comes in, then back at his work. He doesn't seem surprised to see her. Olivia gets the feeling that Sam has known the secret about going where you want even longer than Olivia has.

'I'm reading *The Iliad*. From your list,' she says.

'Good,' Sam says.

'I'm not far into it. There was a summary on the download site though. The Trojan horse – that's the big one they all hide inside, right?'

Sam looks up again and nods.

'I'd only heard that term in computer class before. Trojan horse,' she admits. Sam gives her a momentary smile, skittish and fleeting.

'Me too,' he tells her. 'That's why I wanted to read the story. To know why it was called that.'

'It's a cool name. For a computer thing, or a real thing. All the names in the book are good,' Olivia agrees. 'Do you want my help?'

Sam shrugs, but he makes room for her to join in beside him.

'I like the name Erida best,' he says. 'Of the names in the story. It's a girl's name.'

'I'm not up to her yet. But it's pretty.'

'She's the goddess of hate. She lets out a scream so fierce and bitter that all the soldiers forget everything they used to know – their fathers, their families. All they can think about is doing battle. If I ever got to name a girl, I'd name her Erida.'

'If I got to name a girl,' Olivia offers. 'I'd call her Arcadia. That's from a play.'

'It's not a girl-name, though. It's a place-name.'

Olivia shrugs. 'I like it.'

'Stoppard, right? The play. It's about mathematics.'

'Chaos, yes,' she agrees.

'The ending's sad. I remember that. I didn't think there were any modern stories with sad endings in the legal archives.'

'No.' Olivia shakes her head. 'Not sad. Perfect. Even though you already know that she dies and he goes crazy, that's not where it ends. It ends with them dancing. Whatever comes next, it stops them in that perfect moment. That's the secret to a happy ending. Knowing where to stop.'

Sam gives her a long look, like she's a puzzle he wants to understand. They finish his work without further conversation.

11

Visiting Sam becomes something Olivia looks forward to right from the moment she wakes up in the morning. It gets her through boring classes, through bullies shoving and pushing and calling her nasty things.

It's not the books – though she loves the books and is infinitely grateful for them, and will happily skip buying lunch for the rest of her life in order to afford them – it's Sam himself. Hannah was the first real friend Olivia ever had, and Sam's the only person she's met since who could be the second.

The room where he lives, upstairs from the café, is always a complete mess, but a comfortable mess. His clothes are all soft and worn and made of fine, smooth textures, so all the piles on the floor in his room are nice to sit on.

'I don't like anything rough or itchy or bright,' he explains, frowning as if even the thought of it makes him feel bad.

Olivia, remembering the wool coat left behind in the cell, thinks Sam's attitude is an eminently reasonable one.

Sam's hobby is drawing shapes with many sides, laid out in orthographic projections. The mathematician in her is enchanted by the clean poetry of his lines. The diagrams remind Olivia of honeycombs.

'A three-dimensional shape with twenty sides is an icosahedron,' Sam explains, pointing imperiously at one of the pictures which decorate his walls. His pictures help him with his words, because the desire to explain them to Olivia is strong enough that he makes the effort. 'It has thirty edges and twelve vertices. Twenty triangles all the same size in five rows of four can be folded up to make an icosahedron.'

She likes to watch Sam draw his projections. His movements are so precise, his concentration intense. It's like watching a tailor at work. The creation of a whole from small, exact pieces, placed together with talent and skill.

But more than that, she likes to fight about poetry with him. Maybe that's cliché – being a girly girl, talking about pretty words – but Olivia doesn't care.

Sometimes when they're both lounging on the futon in his room, or sitting on the sidewalk early in the morning before she goes to school, Olivia lets Sam play with her messy, uneven hair. In those moments, she asks him to recite parts of plays and epics, or to tell her what the structures of stories mean.

'The great Greek plays are tragedies,' Sam says, his fingertips smoothing back a loose lock of hair behind her ear. She's resting her head against his shoulder, her reader full of textbooks abandoned on her lap. His T-shirt is soft under her cheek. Olivia wishes that the moment could last forever and ever.

'The tragedy has to come from a terrible error the hero makes. That's what Aristotle says. The word is *hamartia*, which is usually translated as "tragic flaw". But that isn't what it means. It just means one mistake. One mistake that ruins everything.

'Tragedy gives the audience *catharsis* – release, relief. We're healed through the experience of watching characters go through suffering and pain.'

Olivia frowns. 'That's not a very good theory; not for applying across a whole medium. Why do we have to find healing in a story about somebody being broken? Can't we find healing in a story about somebody, you know, *healing*?'

'Howard Barker – he was a British playwright – said that tragedy equips you against lies, but after a musical you're anybody's fool.'

Olivia smacks Sam's chest, making a noise of outrage. 'You can't get away with calling me a fool just by attributing the words to someone else, jerk. And I still say I'm right. Tragedies never feel complete to me. They're stories that don't have a third act.'

'Just because you don't like the ending doesn't mean it's not an ending,' Sam replies, flat-toned but in good humour. It's an old argument, one they enjoy too much to ever agree about.

'Yes it does,' Olivia fires back, sitting up properly so she can look Sam in the eye. 'Sad endings being treated as automatically profound is so sophomoric-'

'To be fair, you *are* a sophomore.'

She ignores the interruption. 'And it's just *wrong*. Things start out all right, then they go bad, and then they're supposed to get *better*. That's how stories are *meant to go*. Otherwise you're ending *Star Wars* with *The Empire Strikes Back*.'

'In tragedy's defence, a lot of people would be perfectly happy if *Star Wars* did exactly that,' Sam jokes, deadpan. 'And tragedies are exactly right, for what they are.'

'But what they are is *wrong*.'

Sam gives a shrug. 'They can't help that.'

12

One afternoon, a whole glut of customers order souvlaki at once. Olivia helps where she can in the kitchen. Even with the extra pair of hands, it's a very hectic hour or so for all of them.

By the end of it she is exhausted and exhilarated, but Sam's a complete wiped out wreck. He sits on the kitchen floor, leaning against the side of the fridge and closing his eyes, his face relaxing as he's soothed by the hum of the motor.

It's almost closing time, and Olivia thinks the other people who work behind the counter can manage the rest of the shift without their help.

'C'mon, let me help you upstairs,' she says, reaching to help him up. Sam shies away from her touch, climbing to his feet on his own and shuffling towards the narrow flight of stairs.

Olivia's worried by how strung-out he is. It's as if dealing with that many people has used up every reserve of energy he had. Sam kicks off his shoes and lies on top of his thin coverlet, his hand making that same nervous-fidgeting flapping movement that he did the first time she came around.

'Are you okay?'

He glances down to see what she's looking at, and gives a weird, nasty-sounding laugh at the sight of his own hands and arms.

'My mother always used to tell me "quiet hands, Sam",' he says, making his voice stern and sharp on the last three words. 'I tried, as much as any five-year-old can. She'd tape my hands and wrists to the arms of chairs, trying to teach me how to keep still, but it…' He closes his eyes, as if the memory is painful

41

enough that he has to brace against its hurt. 'I didn't learn the lesson. Within my first week of starting preschool, the teachers noticed my hands. That tipped them off to look for the rest – and here we are.'

Olivia can't breathe. She can't move, can't speak. Her mouth opens anyway. 'You can't mean–'

'It's a form letter. The escort officer brought it when he came to pick me up. One page, folded into thirds. It looks so *ordinary*.'

There's a shell-shocked wonderment in Sam's words, as if he can't believe the details, even after all this time. '*Dear madam, your son has evidenced a failure to thrive. He is being relocated in order to allow for a more appropriate resource allocation to take place. As compensation, you are entitled to government-supported prenatal and neonatal care for your next pregnancy. Please call the following numbers for further information on this incentive scheme. We wish you better luck in the future.*'

And there it is. *Failure to–*

'You're a thrive,' Olivia whispers.

'It's not catching, don't worry.'

'Fuck you.' She kicks against the side of his bed. 'As if I'd be like that about it.'

'You'd be surprised. People are…' Sam pauses, closing his eyes as he searches for the right word. 'Unpredictable.'

'I should have realised. God, I'm an idiot. I didn't even think about why a kid no older than me was working instead of going to school, or how you had grey market connections, or where your family was or anything. I'm sorry.'

'What're you sorry about? It's good that you didn't think of it. Isn't that supposed to be the ultimate goal for a thrive, to pass undetected? We can even earn integration certificates if we pass tests. I haven't tried to take the tests. I thought it was better to keep going as I was. Not to rock the boat.'

'Fuck.' Olivia doesn't know what else to say.

'Hmm?' Sam is confused by the venom in her reaction. His confusion makes her sadder, more upset.

'It's really fucked up, Sam. You're a *kid*. I couldn't manage if I was shoved out on my own and had to get a job and everything.'

He gives her a crooked smile. 'You're an entirely different circumstance. You've already proved you're worth the investment just by being normal, so it's all right for them to put in the effort of raising you. I wouldn't be a good return prospect on the nurture.'

Olivia didn't think it was a literal thing, when people said being shocked felt like their head was spinning. But it really is just like vertigo. Her feet are bloodless and her head is dizzy. How can this be happening in the world she knows, to someone she cares about?

'I didn't…' She has to swallow twice before she can talk. 'I didn't know that thrives happened in this part of the city.' At school and on TV, she'd always heard that the defects and disorders that thrives had were caused by stuff like radiation leaks or chemicals in the soil, leftover remnants from the Wars. That stuff wasn't supposed to be around in the city anymore. Not in the part Olivia lives in, which has trains and plumbing and schools and everything.

Thrives happened in a blurry, distant land called *somewhere else*. They were something for politicians to make up scare campaigns about and for her parents to discuss over dinner while Olivia pushed her food around her plate and ignored them. Thrives weren't… they weren't *Sam*.

'I'm just lucky that what's wrong with me doesn't stop me from being able to work,' Sam remarks, his voice not quite achieving the nonchalant tone he's obviously going for.

'There's nothing wrong with you,' Olivia snaps in reply before she knows she's going to speak. Anger is like a bullet from a gun, tearing through her so fast that she's ripped apart before she knows the shot's gone off.

Even after Hannah, after the kidnapping, Olivia's world was so *little*, so safe. She never… She never thought…

She doesn't know how to think. The rage inside her, the sheer injustice of Sam lying here alone and miserable, of what that means about every other thrive she's ever heard about, that they weren't monsters or less than human, they were just *kids*, just others like Sam, just *people*.

She wants to cry. At least crying would be a reaction. It's like she's going to explode with the force of what she feels.

Sam's gaze has drifted over to one of the towering stacks of books along the edges of his room, to a decrepit hardcover marked *Encyclopaedia of the Ancient World*.

'It's comparatively gentle. In Sparta, babies that didn't measure up were left on hillsides, or thrown off cliffs. We had a guaranteed place in the shelters to sleep until we were ten. The older ones are kind to the younger ones – children that can eat without too much help almost never starve. A lot of cultures have been far harsher.'

Olivia wants to say that this is the coldest of cold comforts she's ever heard of, but she thinks Sam knows that already. Instead, she tries to steady her breathing, to push down the anger boiling through her, and asks, 'Do you still not want to be touched, or can I get in?'

'No, it's okay. I'm okay now.' He shifts to make what room he can on the narrow mattress.

Olivia climbs in next to him and curls herself against his side, hugging her arm across his chest. She wishes she could travel through time, be with him through every moment of hunger or cold or loneliness. But she can't. He had to go through all of it without her, without anyone. All she can do is be here now.

'There's nothing wrong with you,' she says again, her voice quieter now but no less fierce. Sam strokes her hair, as if she's the one that deserves to be comforted.

13

A few weeks later, when the weather turns too hot to cope with, Olivia gets the idea to sneak into her school's indoor pool at night and swim through the worst of the evening warmth. It's humid but rarely breaks into rain, staying at a horribly uncomfortable in-between of *almost* breaking instead. After a couple of weeks of that, Sam is ready to agree to anything that might offer relief – even a plan that makes Olivia's eyes light up in a way he says is "never a comforting sign".

He's never swum before, so she stays down the shallow end with him, where they can stand on the bottom of the pool and have their heads and shoulders above the surface. Being in the cold, clean water after the sticky and smog-filled afternoon outside makes Olivia so happy that she feels like singing.

She wants to stay at the shallow end and be a good friend. She does. But the allure of the depths is too strong, the thought of ducking her head under and pushing off from the wall and gliding all the way to the other end under the power of a few kicks. Olivia doesn't swim much when the class comes to the pool because she feels gangly and self-conscious and clumsy, but now only Sam is here, so she's not afraid.

She does a few laps, then comes back to him in the shallows. 'Do you want to try? I'll help,' she offers. Sam makes a face.

'We've only been in the water five minutes,' he says. 'Expecting me to do laps already is faster than I'd like to go.'

'Pfft.' Olivia makes a noise of dismissal and splashes the water at him with her hands. 'When I was learning how to swim, my father threw me straight in the deep end.'

'Yes, but your father's an asshole.'

The words make Olivia pause, uncertain about whether it's okay for her to smile at them. Nobody's said that to her since Hannah.

Olivia misses Hannah. Having a new friend in Sam doesn't replace her feelings about her old one. There's room in her heart for both.

She once told Hannah that it'd be nice to see the ocean with her someday. She imagines that, sometimes, the two of them off on an adventure. Maybe Sam can be there too, all three of them living wild on an abandoned island with clean beaches.

No place like that exists in the real world, of course, but that doesn't stop her dreaming.

If they're going to run away to the ocean, though, then first Olivia has to teach Sam to swim.

'Come on,' she says. 'Try to copy what I do.'

14

The next book that Olivia loves, another ratty paperback she buys from Sam, is called *It* and is by somebody named Stephen King. The horror and fear of the story, the unhappy children and the terrible, bloodthirsty clown, are a huge and unexpected comfort to Olivia's hungry heart. The idea of frightening things hiding in the dark is a security blanket for her. Better a nightmare than nobody.

Sam has three ports in his wrist. Olivia has almost never seen anybody with a port before, apart from in movies and shows. And Hannah. Hannah had five.

The ports in movies and shows are mostly prosthetics, stuck on with spirit gum and peeled off when the actors are finished playing. If any actors in the shows and movies have real ports, the ports are hidden with bracelets or watchbands. Paparazzi photographers sneak around trying to get a picture to sell to the entertainment sites for lots and lots of money. Nothing sells as well as shame and secrets. No rich person wants the world to remember how poor they used to be. To have a port is to be marked forever.

'Which is complete nonsense,' Sam points out when she muses aloud on the subject. 'Sixty-five percent of the population is ported, and a full hundred percent use port-interfaced technology in their everyday lives, whether we make use of that aspect of it or not.'

She tells Sam about Hannah, about the whole horrible, thrilling, weird experience that altered something inside Olivia forever, made her who she is now.

'I worry about what Hannah had to do to get away. Who the people she called were, and how much they cost her. It feels like it was my fault she had to do that, because my father hired the men.'

'I'm not going to insult your intelligence by explaining Stockholm Syndrome to you,' he replies in a dry voice, giving her a pointed look. 'But even accounting for that, feeling guilty because you got rescued from being kidnapped is pretty outrageous.'

Olivia sighs. 'Shut up.'

'She probably didn't call anyone. I bet if you'd asked to see the phone logs, it would have been a dead number.'

'No, it was definitely someone. She told them her name was Lissa, and then that's what the lady at the hospital called her.'

'She would have used a phrase or word, a trigger that connected the call to a monitoring station. That's how spies do it, isn't it? And government agencies. The machinery picks up the trigger and starts listening in.'

'Oh.' Olivia thinks hard, trying to remember Hannah's hoarse, rapid words. 'She called someone "little red riding hood". That might have been it. So that clicked the connection on, and then she pretended to be talking while someone listened, and had to trust that they'd understand and help her?'

'Yeah.' Sam nods. 'I hear about things like that sometimes, from my suppliers. I never use them. Reliability like that – knowing for almost certain that someone will come pick you up on nothing more than a hospital name muttered down the phone ten minutes before the needed rescue – that comes at very, very high prices, from what I hear. It would have to. I don't want anything to do with that.'

Olivia's stomach is leaden, cold and heavy. She wishes she knew what happened to Hannah. If she wound up safe and okay. She may never know for sure, and this new piece of information – the first she's had since it all happened – is nothing but bad news.

Late that night, instead of staying up with a book as usual,

Olivia lies in bed and screws up as much courage as she can find. This is so dumb. What's she going to say? So, so dumb.

She punches a random number into her phone and hopes she isn't about to wake up someone. There are way more numbers than phones, right? So this has a good chance of working.

Before anyone can answer, she takes a breath and blurts: 'Little red riding hood! Uh, I hope that's still the right words. I guess it probably isn't, since Ha–, Ah, Lissa used it in front of people. But, um, if you're listening, don't make her pay a lot or anything, okay? It was my fault she got caught in it. So if there's a way for you to give the bill to me instead, if you can find me, do that please. And if you talk to her tell her I'm sorry, and that I, um, tell her...'

Olivia can't think of anything to say, and the phone is only silent empty air beside her ear. She ends the call, and wants to cry.

15

Sometimes Olivia and Sam watch movies together, making a game of finding the absolute outer limits of what's available in the download stores. Today Sam's managed to find Stanley Kubrick's *Lolita*, which Olivia has to admit is going to be an impossible act to follow.

They're up to the scene where Humbert Humbert is lying in his bathtub and a neighbour makes token overtones towards paying for Charlotte's funeral. Humbert Humbert accepts the offer and the man's face falls. Sam laughs.

'That's me. That moment,' he says to Olivia. 'That's the closest anything has come to articulating my manifesto.'

She scowls at him. 'You can't take a manifesto from Humbert Humbert. Don't be gross.' She pokes him above the knee, hard, with the toe of one foot. 'And that scene's not even political anyway. You're full of crap.'

'It's political like graffiti is political, or punk music is. It's political insofar as it demonstrates the fragility of the social construct. The guy was relying on Humbert fulfilling his part of the expected dialogue and saying that the guy didn't have to pay for the funeral. But Humbert didn't say that and now the guy is fucked.'

'You're comparing that to punk and graffiti? Those things *are* political. This is just dark satire; and that's not even touching on the fact that *you* aren't *remotely* punk.'

'Dark satire is punk, fuck you.' He rolls his eyes at her. 'You're so literal all the time. How can you love abstract numbers? I'm *appalling* at metaphors and I'm still better at this than you. Don't give me that look.'

'What look?'

'That look you get when you think I need teaching about how to be a person. You turn into such a condescending bitch.'

Offended, Olivia sits up properly. 'Wow, fuck *you*. You and your completely toothless definition of what punk is.'

'I didn't...' Sam sighs. 'I'm not saying I'm a *dissident*. I'm not. I don't care about changing anything. I just don't care about adhering to it either.'

'You can't live like the rules are for other people, Sam,' she says. 'That's how bad stuff happens to people, thinking like that.'

Nightmare images flit through her head of guns and bloodied masks. She's seen what happens to criminals: they wind up dead on the floor of a cold little room, or vanishing off into the dark like Hannah.

'You'd be happier if you stopped trying to be part of the "other people" that the rules are for. You don't even agree with those rules; why the hell do you put so much effort into acting like you do?' he snipes back at her.

The words sting and she flinches.

'Because it would be *easier*. You think I *like* being so hungry for new weird books all the time? You think I *want* that? I'd do *anything* to be happy the way normal people are, with normal people stuff!' she yells at him.

It's lucky that nobody else is home at her house except for the two of them, at least not in the same wing of the building as her bedroom. The shouting won't carry as far as the kitchen where the servants are.

'No you wouldn't! You hate them and you hate their horrible rules!' he yells back, and she hates him so much for knowing her so well, for knowing the darkest of her secrets. 'My question is, do you hate them for being unfair, or do you hate yourself for not being what they demand you try to be?'

51

Sam points in the direction of her en-suite bathroom. 'I saw that tub of moisturiser you've got in there. Skin-lightening cream. That's *so fucked up*, Olivia. Why would you *do* that?'

She wilts, anger going out of her and the empty space it leaves behind flooding with black despair.

'Because, because I hate the game, and I desperately want to be among the winners; both, at once! Maybe you've never cared to play at all, but I do. I'm so, um, so *raw*, and all I want to be is *refined*. I want to be petite and delicate but I'm tall and loud and I like numbers and I like reading and I like *you*, and I'm supposed to–'

And then, mortifyingly, she starts to cry. She goes into the bathroom and closes the door, sitting with her back against it as she gulps and sobs and turns into a giant snotty mess for a few minutes. She isn't totally certain why she's so upset. It's just that everything is *wrong*, or *she's* wrong, or *something*. Every day she feels more like she can't breathe properly.

'I turned off the movie,' Sam says to her through the door. 'Come back out and we'll watch awful TV together and make fun of how shitty everyone is.'

Olivia gives a snuffly laugh. 'Okay. Gimme a sec.'

She washes her face and then stares at the tub of cream. She wants so much to be pretty, to be the daughter her mother wishes she was. Being a disappointment is horrible.

But if she keeps on doing stuff like putting lightening cream on her face, what message does that send to Sam? That every little imperfection or weirdness or difference that a person has should be wiped away, burned down to nothing wherever possible? What's that say to someone whose whole *self* is deemed to be inferior by those standards?

She drops the container into the trash and goes back out to join him. The TV's showing one of those public safety announcements about how ports should always be covered during "intimate contact".

'Do you think there's anything they can't make grim and

frightening?' Olivia remarks, sitting close to Sam. She's grateful when he doesn't tell her she's a melodramatic jackass for the crying fit.

'It's funny, isn't it,' Sam muses. 'That something made to turn people into products, like the ports, brings us closer to one another as humans. You know why they have those PSAs, right?'

'Yeah, I hear stuff at school. If you have your ports open while you're, you know, doing it, then it can almost be telepathy. This one girl swears she used to date a guy with ports and she says it worked on her even though she doesn't have any. Just having his against her skin was enough.'

Olivia can't help but think that it sounds romantic, being connected to another person like that. She doesn't care about the sex part of it, but the thought of having another mind touch hers is sort of beautiful. Maybe she wouldn't be so lonely, if she could have that.

'It's not romantic,' Sam says dryly. Olivia knows he hasn't read her mind. He simply knows her too well. 'People might think it is, if they never had to use their ports all that much for energy-harvesting or other real tasks. You know how overwhelming social media can get sometimes, with everyone talking about themselves all at once? It's that, but inside your head and in your bones.'

'Ick.'

'Exactly.'

A news story comes on the TV, this one about new zoning laws around the rebuilt ruins and some crackpot with a petition to ban thrives from the area. Sam's jaw clenches, the vein ticking visibly under the skin of his throat. Olivia scrabbles to find something to say, to distract him from the poison onscreen.

'Is it... is it true that sometimes you can hear people's thoughts, even people without ports, once you're ported, though?' she asks. She thinks it would be all right if Sam could see inside her head. She has no secrets from him. She can't imagine that she ever would.

He licks his palm, a long stripe from the heel of his wrist to the tips of his fingers, and rests it on top of her hand.

'Eugh! Warn someone before you do that. Gross,' Olivia objects, glaring at him. Sam ignores her grumbling.

'Think of something,' he instructs her. 'Concentrate hard.'

She thinks of the Mandelbrot set in her visual mathematics textbook. Sam's mouth curves in a sudden smile, and she feels a spark in her brain, a *zap*. It's like touching tinfoil to a tooth filling, and startles a shocked laugh out of her.

'The term *fractal* derives from the latin *fractus*, meaning fractured, or broken,' Sam says.

'Holy shit!' Olivia laughs again. 'Are you fucking serious right now?'

Sam nods, then shrugs one shoulder. 'Ideas like that aren't too hard. Words are easy. Feelings are harder, but I don't know if that's how all ports work or if that's just because I'm me. You'd need to ask someone else, and compare their experience, to know for certain.'

When they get bored of the crap on TV, they wind up sitting on the carpet while Olivia makes a listless attempt at her homework and Sam reads one of his books about ancient Greece.

She's got a study sheet that she's meant to complete for health class. They're learning self-defence and it's all pretty gross and stupid. The teacher spent more time talking to the all-girl class about making sure not to give mixed signals or dress provocatively than he did showing them how to stomp their heel down on an attacker's foot, or what the weakest and most vulnerable parts to aim for were.

When Olivia had finally hit her exasperation limit and put her hand up, she'd asked the teacher, 'Is this stuff about clothes and "asking for it" really the best stuff for keeping us safe? Shouldn't you be doing an all-boy class about not thinking those things are an invitation in the first place?'

One of Olivia's head tormenters giggled and whispered to the girl beside her, who glanced at Olivia and started laughing too.

'Sir,' the first bully said, her glossy mouth a snide frown. 'I think Olivia needs remedial classes. We all know she failed the practical exam on not getting grabbed.'

Now, trying to concentrate on her homework, Olivia remembers the taunt and her fists curl tight in impotent fury. She'd love to see all of those horrid jerks at school go through what she went through. They could see how funny they thought it was to crack jokes about it after they had to give up food when they were hungry so they could get stuff to make their eyes stop hurting. After they'd seen dead bodies so fresh that blood was still coming out of the bullet holes.

Olivia shoves her homework away, too sick and angry to do any more.

Sam glances up, but doesn't ask her what's wrong.

'Can I interrupt your reading?'

'In the strictest sense, yes, I'm sure you're more than capable of that.'

'Very funny.'

'I thought so, yes.' Sam closes his book and places it on the floor beside him. 'What's wrong?'

'Doesn't matter.' Olivia sighs. 'Do you ever wish that the sky would open up and a chunk of moon-rock would plummet down and land right on the head of someone you hate?'

'That's a pretty *deus ex machina* solution to the problem.'

'A what?'

'It means "god from the machine". The term's Latin, but it's from the Greek. Onstage in plays, the actors playing gods would appear by being lifted by this special machinery designed for the task. So the term describes when something completely improbable and unexpected shows up out of nowhere to solve things.'

'Sounds like bull to me,' offers Olivia. 'It's one thing for me to daydream it, but to use it as a way to resolve actual stories is pretty lazy.'

'Nietzsche thought so too. He said that the reason the Greek playwrights started relying on it was because the trends in staging had stopped putting gross comedy skits and musicians in between the dark, serious stories. Nietzsche's idea was that without the music and crazy stuff, audiences had no way left to cope with tragedy. They couldn't give themselves over to the catharsis without songs and laughter, it was just too fucked up and hopeless. And so, with no other way to purge the emotional darkness of sad stories, the writers had to make the comfort come out of nowhere: the god out of the machine.'

16

Olivia's dad buys one of the new houses that're popping up where the ruins used to be.

'Maybe you can live in it when you're grown-up and have a husband,' Olivia's mother says.

'Don't be stupid,' her father replies. 'Her husband will have houses of his own for her.'

Everyone at school gets obsessed with the developments too, about what new shops are going to open and how big the screens at the new movie theatre are rumoured to be. A petition goes up on all the social networks about changing the proposed zoning laws so that residents can have category 2 exotic pets instead of just the category 1 domestic kind.

A kid in Olivia's class – he's not one of the mean ones, he's never pushed her down the stairs or called her a shitty name – makes a crack about how he'll sign any petition that lets people keep thrives as pets, so long as they're sexy ones.

Olivia spends three patient, vicious hours hacking into every nook and cranny of his online presence and locking him out of it permanently. The revenge makes her feel better for a minute or two, but she knows it hasn't solved any of the problems that led him to saying it in the first place.

She tells herself that it'll be okay. There isn't going to be any ban on thrives. Thrives have most of the same rights as other people. The developments won't have any effect on Sam. Stupid jokes on social media won't have any effect on Sam.

Olivia pays more attention to things people say than she ever has before. She does it in the hope that she'll put her mind at ease, but it doesn't work out that way. Every joke and nasty comment she hears makes her angrier, more afraid. She doesn't know how anyone can think that those things stay harmless for very long.

17

At breakfast one morning, Olivia's parents are talking about a news story while Olivia pushes her food around her plate and tries to ignore them.

'Some big hot-shots are buying ambulances, taking out the interiors, and doing them up like limousines inside,' Olivia's mother says. 'When they want to go somewhere fast, they get the driver to put the siren on and all the other cars get out of their way.'

Her father laughs loudly, slapping the table with an open palm.

'That's a way to dodge the traffic!' he guffaws. 'That's the kind of clever thinking I need to hire more of.'

Olivia drops her fork, letting it clatter sharply against the bone china of her plate. 'That's *disgusting*.'

'It's survival of the fittest. The strong eat the weak. That's how nature works,' her father sneers.

'That's not even what survival of the fittest *means*,' Olivia sneers right back. 'That would be stupid, if the natural order was for bullies to always win. Of course *you* would think that the world was that horrible.' She lets out a mean little laugh.

Her father is livid. 'No school lunches for you this week. No money at all. That'll teach you to have some respect for me and the work I do to provide for this family. You're a disgrace and a disappointment. Get out of here.'

She goes, feeling bad about the outburst, though not very. What an awful thing for her father to laugh about. What a bleak way to see the world.

Skipping lunch is no big deal. She does it all the time. It's Sam's afternoon off, so he meets her at the gate when classes end and they walk through the busy, noisy neighbourhood with no particular destination in mind. He's in a quiet mood, but after the argument that morning Olivia doesn't especially feel like talking. They chat about her physics assignment, and the most recent water restrictions, and other stuff that doesn't mean anything.

When the light starts to go golden and evening's on the way, Olivia sighs. 'I guess we should both get home.'

'I guess,' Sam agrees. His hand is fluttering, but when he notices he stills it. Olivia frowns. He doesn't have to do that around her. She thought he knew that.

'Oh. Here.' He drops his backpack to the ground, rummaging through it before handing a paper package to her. It's the familiar dimensions of a carefully wrapped novel.

'Oh, but I can't pay for this. No money this week, not even for lunches,' Olivia says, passing the book back to him with a pang of regret. 'Thanks, though. I'll grab it off you as soon as I can.'

'That's okay,' Sam says. 'I want you to have it. It can be a present.'

It's called *Lord of the Flies* and, as usual, Olivia skips sleeping that night in favour of getting lost in the words. It's about a group of children sent away from the Wars, who end up stranded and alone on an island. They try to live well and decently, but soon enough everything goes wrong and they become wilder and more dangerous. They give in to their savage natures.

Her favourite character is Piggy, because he wears glasses like her and because he cares so much what his aunt would have to say about everything. She isn't surprised when he meets a bad end. For all that her father is wrong about the nature of evolution, Olivia knows as well as anyone that life is not always kind, especially to the weak.

No wonder Hannah was so exasperated with Olivia, when Olivia said that books were boring. Books are the *opposite* of boring. They make her want to cry sometimes, when sad things happen like poor Piggy's fate. Other times, they make her want to laugh, or cheer, or fight.

Books are their own kind of telepathy, a sparking zap that passes words from one brain to another.

On the inside back cover of the book is a handwritten message. Olivia recognises Sam's penmanship immediately, from the list of book titles he gave her the very first time they met. His writing is very small and very neat, nothing like the reckless scrawl of Olivia's own. She never needs to write anything by hand in class; to say she's out of practice is an understatement. But Sam's handwriting is as neat as printing.

Olivia

I've been through this before. After petitions come protests, after protests come attacks. I'm not sticking around until I get my eyes blackened or my fingers broken, or worse, by someone who wants people like me out of their area. The ruins will be a luxury neighbourhood soon. By then it might be too late for me to get away safely. So I'm leaving now.

Don't come back to the cafe. I'll be gone before you get to the end of this book. I dislike goodbyes. I hope you aren't angry for me avoiding it this way

I'll miss you.

Sam

Sam will be gone, like Hannah's gone. One moment Olivia's hand was holding hers and then they were pulled apart, two kids in a crowd. Now Sam will be the same – a vanishing shape in the dark. Olivia will be left alone again.

She walks to the train station near her house in the rapidly rising dawn light. The pollution makes the sky brilliant at this time of day, oil-slick greens and pinks and blues like the wings of a giant beetle overhead. Olivia breathes in deep and imagines the colours coating her lungs, spreading emerald and sapphire and ruby disease all through her. Carmine, that's the one that's made from beetles, isn't it?

The former ruins are dark outside the window as she rides to

61

the stop near the souvlaki place, but that's because it's too early for people to have their lights on yet. It's all built up now. The empty space is gone.

Olivia doesn't think it's right to call it rebuilding, like everyone else does. It's not rebuilding. They're destroying too much for it to be called that.

Sam's upstairs, packing a few of his things into a knapsack. Olivia looks at all the things he's leaving behind – his drawings, his books, his comfortable worn old bedding and clothes in their haphazard little piles – and she has to swallow hard before she can trust herself to speak in a level voice.

'I'm coming with you.'

Sam pivots on his heel, staring at her in surprise. Olivia's a bit offended by that. Did he truly think that she'd accept his note without any reaction, without coming here to see him?

'That's stupid,' he tells her.

She shrugs. 'Okay. Probably you're right. I'm still coming.'

18

They catch the train to the central transit hub. Olivia's only been to the inner city a handful of times. Even in the morning sunshine, the ground level is so dim that all the street lights are on. The buildings seem to go up for miles, packed in so close and dense that the air is stale and thin at the bottom.

Lines of drying clothes stretch between the skyscrapers on the lowest few dozen floors, which Olivia thinks is wishful thinking by whoever put them there. *Outdoors* and *indoors* don't mean much this low, except that the outdoors is more likely to be polluted.

Higher up are the greenhouse walkways, their round glass sides fogged with condensation, ghostly shapes and shades of plants visible through the misty surface. Olivia wonders what it's like to live up there, in apartments with natural light and clean new air, windows that aren't designed to open and nature recreated in long bright hallways suspended over the dark drop to the ground.

'Living here must be strange,' she muses. Sam shrugs.

They catch another train, this one old and noisy and rocking as it moves out to the industrial zones. Olivia watches the neighbourhoods go by outside her window until the motion makes her sick and she has to close her eyes.

The city is so big. It goes on forever. Olivia's never thought about that. How it's actually just one small bit of the world.

Her parents only left it once in their whole lives, when they all went on holiday to the sea. Olivia might have lived the rest of her life without leaving it again – and might still, since the industrial zones are well within city limits, and who knows where they're going to end up after that?

'What I've done in the past at a time like this,' Sam explains as they reach the station at the end of the line, 'is find a factory and work there for three to six months or so. If we're careful, we'll earn enough to live on for a while. I can contact my suppliers, get new stock, and we can live like how I was at the cafe.'

Even though it sucks that Sam's life has been so shitty that he's had to learn this stuff, Olivia is grateful that he knows what he's doing. If she was on her own, she wouldn't know what the hell to do.

Of course, without Sam she might never have had a proper reason to run away at all. She'd have just kept on being miserable, and feeling there was no way out except to try to be more like the people who seemed happy with that kind of life.

They stop at a public communication terminal before they look for work, so that they can buy some food and Sam can message all his contacts to explain that he's going on hiatus.

Olivia fires up a messenger program on another monitor, punching in a few tweaks so her location won't be recorded. She's so glad that Hannah's breezy electronic vandalism of her reader showed her that hacking isn't such a big deal. Without her little cache of self-taught tricks, Olivia might not have thought of doing this. It feels important that she does this, though, so it's good that she knows how to go about it.

The message she sends her parents isn't long. She promises them that she's safe and hasn't been kidnapped again. She tells her father that it has nothing to do with him punishing her. There was just somewhere that she needed to go, and that there wasn't any choice about. She's okay.

Olivia thinks about signing off by saying that she loves them, but doing that seems cruel when she's just told them that she's run away, so in the end she just signs her name and sends the message.

If her eyes are a little redder than usual behind her glasses as they leave the terminal, Sam doesn't remark on it.

19

They find a factory very quickly; all of the places they pass are looking for workers.

The minimum age for work is supposed to be sixteen, and Olivia is barely fifteen, but nobody cares. Nobody asks to see her ID, or Sam's, and while Olivia is tall and lanky for her age, Sam is the opposite. Olivia's not certain if he's fifteen yet.

Who they are doesn't matter; only that they do the work given to them. They're cogs now, not people.

The factory makes shoes and purses out of fake tan leather and fake grey crocodile skin. The girl workers sleep eight to a room for the most part, but Olivia wants to be near Sam so she lives in the same dorm as him, twelve kids no older than they are, all on bunks that crowd in close even near the toilet and the sink in the corner. Everything's dirty and everything smells bad.

The canteen food is meat or vegetables, plus rice. They don't get meal breaks at the same time because their shifts don't match. Olivia works twelve hours a day, with one break of twenty minutes after the first six hours. Sam works fourteen hours with two meal breaks of fifteen minutes each.

At night, when the air is too cold to bear and the shivering stops them from sleeping, they huddle close and put their blankets over both of them together. Sometimes that's enough.

Despite their differing builds, features, and colouring, Olivia and Sam are starting to look as similar as siblings. Both are losing puppy fat, gaining a gaunt and hollow cast to their features. Their skins have a matching ashy undertone, their eyes an almost fevered brightness.

Nobody notices. It's normal for factory kids to look like that.

When sharing a bunk and blankets isn't enough to warm them, Olivia and Sam creep down to the loading docks to run around. It reminds Olivia of the night they went swimming, when the weather was warm. That already feels as though it happened to two other people, in some other far-off life.

Often she wakes up alone, even if she fell asleep with Sam beside her, because he signs up for generator shifts in the early, early morning hours. He's given a glucose drink and a cable, and he has to swallow the drink and then port himself in, charging the power grid for the coming day's work.

'Some people do nothing but those shifts. It pays well,' he tells Olivia, but no matter how often they argue about it, she never lets him switch to doing more grid-time and less assembly-time. She's seen the people he's talking about, the ones who do nothing but port shifts. They look more dead than alive.

The number Sam already does are bad for him. By the time he's finished one, and then his regular hours on the assembly line, he's more wrung-out and overloaded than Olivia ever saw him at the souvlaki place. He flinches away from any touch, and on those evenings Olivia lets him have both their blankets and she sits up next to him, worried and sad.

20

'Talk to me.'

It's a half-hour before midnight, time stretching thin in the dark. Everyone else in the dormitory is asleep, or out doing overtime.

Olivia can't see Sam's face clearly with the light this low, but his voice sounds stronger and less pained than it did earlier in the night. Something tense and tight in her heart loosens a fraction.

'I liked *The Odyssey* better than *The Iliad*,' she says, keeping her voice soft. 'I guess I'm more interested in journey-stories than in war-stories. War-stories are full of hating and hurting, even when they're beautifully told. I'd rather hear about what happened after. How they found their way home. Do you want me to keep going?'

'Yes.'

'Okay. Well,' Olivia tries to think of what else to say on the subject. 'I like *The Odyssey*, but I think it's weird. It's a story within a story, and then inside that story they stop to listen while people talk about other stories. And it takes so long for him to get home. His kid is all grown up before they even meet. That's depressing.'

'It's not depressing. It's a delayed pay-off. Sometimes an ending is happier because of how hard the characters have had to work for it.'

'You know, I'm starting to think you just hate the idea of anything ever being easy,' Olivia says dryly. She shivers, looking around at the darkness of the room full of breathing bodies and not quite enough air. 'Do you ever get claustrophobic in here?'

'It's reminding you of where you were held when you were kidnapped.'

'No mind-reading, little robot mouse. You're meant to be resting.'

'Didn't need to read your mind. I know it off by heart.'

21

Olivia sometimes wonders what she would be like if she'd never run away. Who she'd have become, instead of this exhausted, strung-out version of who she used to be.

Then she remembers that if she hadn't run away, there'd be no Sam in her life anymore, and the daydreams fall away in a sick smear of fear at what could have been.

She does her best to stay on-task, to remember how serious their situation is. She knows it's serious. She does. But Olivia's inherently Olivia, no matter how serious things might be, and that means that she's sometimes a daydreamer and sometimes distracted, and that means she fucks up sometimes and gets things wrong.

Eventually, the reprimands for her mistakes escalate from being screamed at by the floor manager and having her wages docked. She winds up in the office of a higher-up manager.

She loses track of which manager is responsible for managing which other manager. It's one huge daisy chain of busywork, everyone minding everyone else's business and everyone pissed off at Olivia because she isn't meticulous enough about quality control.

'You're such a stupid fucking idiot I should put you down in the port rooms, sit you down and siphon off your energy for the batteries. At least then you might be some fucking use for a change!' the manager screams at her. He has spittle at the corners of his mouth and tiny red veins at the corners of the whites of his eyes, so Olivia thinks that whatever she did wrong or forgot to do completely must have been more important than the usual screw-ups.

'You can try,' she answers back, too tired to keep her tongue in check. 'But I won't do you much good, seeing as how I've never been ported.'

The manager's eyes widen. He wraps his clammy, meaty hand around her forearm and inspects her unscarred wrist for himself.

Olivia waves the fingers of her now-raised hand at him. 'Howdy.'

He lets go of her as abruptly as he'd taken hold, and sends her out of the room without any more insults or blame. He seems embarrassed. It's super weird, but Olivia's never dissected and tried to understand the motivations for people's weirdness in the past. That's even truer now that she's so tired and miserable all the time. She has no energy left to wonder about anything, especially not things related to cranky, angry managers.

That same week, Olivia is transferred from her spot on the factory floor to a job in the computer centre. She tries to explain that she doesn't know the first thing about computers, but everyone else in the computer centre smiles, pats her on the arm and says she'll get the hang of it soon enough.

Sam's no help, either. When Olivia explains what's going on, about how she's wound up with a job that she doesn't know how to do, but that nobody seems to care about that, Sam shrugs.

'You weren't very good at the assembly line, either. It doesn't make much difference if you're going to be unskilled in a new role.'

And sure, that's true, but that doesn't mean it's *useful*. It doesn't explain why not having ports earned Olivia a promotion.

She's sure that's what's done it, and that's *so fucked up*, because Olivia likes having a higher wage and being able to sit down and not breathe in chemicals all day in a giant, noisy room, but it's not like she *deserves* it more than any of the other factory kids just because she grew up differently.

She's no different to any of them now, that's for sure: just as poor and desperate and anonymous and disposable. She's not some better class of person because her wrists are free of marks.

So now she works in computers. Surprisingly, she picks it up soon enough. She enters the data she's given, and prints out the data she's told to print, and mails the messages she's told to mail. It's not that different from the assembly line, except now when she fucks up she can press "undo" and nobody needs to know.

It gets boring very, very quickly. That's why she starts hacking again.

22

The first thing Olivia learned about sneaking around inside technology was that the extreme level of security pervading everything official in the city was, by its very nature, incredibly dumb. The controls were designed to be so stringent that nobody had bothered to finesse the filtering systems which governed them.

She found this out the same way as most other people who knew about it: she happened to be present for a pig test.

After Hannah but before Sam, Olivia had been searching for more fairy tales to download. She'd been trying to think of how to increase her chances of finding the rare unsanitised collections that she particularly liked. If she was too obvious, she risked drawing attention to the fact that the stories existed, and that would have resulted in their deletion from the archives, and who knew what personal consequences for Olivia herself.

She'd been aimlessly looking, and as she was scrolling through a thread about anthology recommendations, a new post popped up with nothing in it but a snapshot of a piglet.

The conversation went dead for half a minute, then suddenly everyone was posting at once.

House of bricks confirmed!

Niiiiice.

fucking finally now can someone please help me find american gothic tales ed was joyce carol oates

Over the next few hours, and the days that followed, Olivia discovered the secret world of censor evasion. She hadn't known how it worked, or the significance of the piglet picture, until she got to know Sam, and he explained it to her.

'Because so much information is generated every day, the filters the city uses can't monitor everything at all times. Instead, they run on an algorithm that's designed to point them at the places where they're most likely to find content that needs to be blocked. With me so far?'

Olivia had given him an unimpressed look. When Sam had waited, not picking up on the cue, Olivia answered properly. 'Yeah, I'm with you. Algorithms are a thing I know really well. I like things like that.'

'Right. You like maths. I forgot. So, while nobody can ever be certain if the site they're visiting is being watched at a given moment, they can make a fair guess by learning the rough pattern that the filters are using. The pig is a final double-check before people talk freely. If the filter turns out to be watching them after all, the pig picture won't load. It registers as naked human skin to the content algorithm, and gets automatically deleted before it shows up. So if you can see the pig, the filter can't see you.'

It's such a hilariously dumb, simple thing that Olivia can't help but love it. Such a sweet, silly thing, telling her that she's safe to speak freely and seek the things she wants without trying to think up likely code-words that others could be using in place of the real terminology.

Knowing what she already knows about dipping below the surface of the sanctioned web, it doesn't take her long to work out how to dodge the factory's local security and get out into broader connectivity. It's like drawing a deep breath after being at high altitude; she is almost drunk on the freedom of being able to find whatever her heart desires.

Well, almost. What she wants most is to find something better, somewhere safer, for her and Sam. She'll take what she can in the meantime.

It's dumb to miss paperbacks as much as she does, to wish that she had access to books that she could touch and hold. But that's a tiny pang compared to the thrill of being able to get new words again, any words she wants and not just the sanctioned trash available in the factory dispensaries.

Olivia seeks out message boards and chats. Most of the other hackers think they're tough and interesting on account of the fact that they can choose to be rude to one another and say outrageous things. Olivia's got no time for them, or for their imagined hardness. She finds better chats, better boards, hunting the wilds of the grey web until she finds conversations worth having.

She gives herself a dozen names with a single definition between them: flighty, fickle, capricious. Young. All of the things she had to leave behind, the things she might have been if the world had ever given her a proper chance to try them. Olivia calls herself Soubrette, for the pretty, silly girls of the French stage. Or she's Dalal, which is Arabic and means much the same thing. Or Tannaz, the Persian version, or Gamze, the Turkish, or Gery from Old English. A dozen names, two dozen, three.

Behind these new digital masks, she seeks out information.

Soubrette: where do grey web nodes spring from?

Pancake: Any server space they can steal

Pancake: The magnetic pulses wipe anything outside city limits, which means no access for outliers and means no hosting either. So it's all stolen space.

Trixy: I can teach you how to turn your factory into a node. You could channel a lot through there.

Soubrette: Nope

Soubrette: No dice.

Soubrette: The people who fuel the batteries are overworked as it is without us making them power our libraries and boards too.

Soubrette: Show me how to set up a remote one in a solar tower or nuclear area instead.

Trixy: You're weird

Soubrette: I'll take that as a compliment.

23

One evening, the cafeteria has small cups of stale, chewy popcorn. It's coated in slightly rancid synthetic butter and is being sold for an exorbitant price, but Olivia doesn't hesitate before buying servings for herself and Sam. Popcorn is frivolous and useless and fun – all the things being young is supposed to contain. She hasn't felt young for a long time, and doubts that Sam has either, but she is going to make them pretend even if it kills them.

They eat their treats while sitting out in the loading bay. The air has a rotten edge to it tonight, like garbage left out in sunlight for days, despite the fact that not much sunlight makes its way to ground level in this part of town.

Sam's in a quiet mood, even by Sam standards. He keeps running his thumb back and forth over the band on his wrist, gazing thoughtfully at it.

Olivia throws a piece of popcorn at his head, then another one after the first fails to attract his attention.

On the third strike, which bounces off the shell of Sam's ear, Sam looks at her with a poisonous glare. Olivia grins at him.

'Boo.'

He looks away again. Any other time, Olivia would give up at this point, write the evening off as a loss and Sam's behaviour as typical Sam-ness. But as he turns away, she sees a thumb-shaped bruise below the edge of his collar at the nape of his neck.

'What's that from? On your neck?' she asks, putting the rest of the popcorn on the ground beside her and forgetting about it.

'It doesn't matter.'

'Like hell it doesn't. If it didn't matter, you'd tell me.'

'I'm not a fucking infant you need to babysit.' Sam gets to his feet and walks back towards the door into the factory. Olivia scrambles to follow him, grabbing his arm.

'This isn't about *babysitting*, you asshole. If I pulled this bull on you, you'd want to know how I got hurt, wouldn't you?'

He lets out a long, frustrated sigh. 'I'm handling it. You don't need to worry. If I need your help, I'll tell you. Is that enough?'

It's nowhere near enough, but Olivia knows that if she keeps pushing, it'll make him more annoyed and less likely to tell her anything. For now, she's got no choice but to wait, and to hope that Sam will come to her with the problem in his own time.

24

Soubrette: just us two online today?

Trixy: Pancake was on earlier

Trixy: might be back later

Soubrette: It's you I wanted to talk to actually.

Trixy: ?

Soubrette: You knew I was in a factory.

Trixy: if you're trying to stay anon you're gonna have to do a lot more security

Soubrette: No idc about that

Soubrette: you're good at finding out stuff

Soubrette: can you find people?

Soubrette: I'm trying to find someone. She used to be a masker.

Soubrette: I don't know if she still is.

Trixy: Nobody's a masker now

Trixy: they're all long dead.

Trixy: you need a Ouija board

Trixy: not a hacker.

Soubrette: wait

Soubrette: I wanna find someone else

Soubrette: They were like a go-to person

Soubrette: If you were in serious trouble. They helped you get out.

Trixy: I'll need more information than that. Can you be more specific?

Soubrette: They might have been called little red riding hood

Trixy has invited you into secure chat.

WARNING: Do not accept secure chats from people you don't know. Do not accept secure chats while ported to your machine.

Trixy: you're looking for Carabosse.

Soubrette: is that their real name or another aka

Trixy: that's the real name.

Soubrette: so how do I find Carabosse then?

Soubrette: or are you gonna say something spooky and dumb like 'Carabosse finds you'

Soubrette: you're deleting those exact words right now aren't you

Soubrette: ?

Trixy doesn't say anything else for the rest of the day, and Pancake doesn't come back. Olivia has a vague twinge of her old, pallid fear that used to weigh her down right after the kidnapping – the gnawing worry that someone is about to burst through a door and shoot her for something stupid and reckless she's got caught up in.

But it's a familiar, worn-out fear, and it's hard to muster the energy to give it new vitality. Nobody gives a shit what some computer tech at a shady factory is doing in a chat room, especially with no images or files being exchanged.

Still, it's not entirely a surprise when, a few days later, a window pops up on one of her screens and a row of text types itself into the little blank box.

Your password was genuinely challenging. Congratulations.

Olivia hits the soundproofing switch on her cubicle, raising the partitions around her desk to the low ceiling, and sticks her headset on.

We can talk voice-to-voice if you prefer. I've put the walls up, she types in reply.

'Hi,' a very electronic approximation of a voice tunes flatly in her ear. She gives a start of surprise, then hears a burst of staticky sort-of-laughter.

'Sorry. Didn't mean to get you off-guard.'

'No problem,' she says with a small laugh of her own. 'So who are you?'

'We have a mutual acquaintance. I'm here to check that your intentions towards them are good.' The timbre of the generated voice makes the words sound particularly formal.

Olivia puts on the cheesiest, most wholesome tone she can muster. 'I promise to have her home by midnight, sir. We're just going to the drive-in and the malt shop. No funny stuff, I promise.'

There's a blart of static, as though the electronic voice tried and failed to translate another laugh. Then the voice asks, 'You're looking for a masker?'

'Yeah. She was a red rabbit.'

'Why do you think Red Rabbit was female?'

'You can talk in your real voice,' says Olivia. 'They give us secure lines.'

'This is my real voice,' the caller replies in the same digitised tones. 'Answer the question.'

'Okay, okay. I think Red Rabbit is female because one of us had to cough up a piece of information to prove we're not just some spy spinning bullshit in order to catch the other. You've got me on the back foot because you know how to find me and I don't know how to find you, so I thought it was fair that I tell you something to prove I'm on the level,' she replies.

There's a pause, long enough that Olivia wonders if the mystery caller is still there. Then the static flares again, and they speak.

'Have you heard of the method of teaching a child to swim that involves throwing the child in the deep end?'

'Yes...' Olivia responds, certain that she's not going to like whatever comes next.

Another burst of robotic laughter in her ear. 'Fourteen data packets are encrypted into your terminal. Put together they'll give you a password. If you don't enter the password in the next four hours, your computer is going to explode. If you fall behind in your regular tasks, your computer is going to explode. Have fun.'

The line goes silent. Olivia pulls off her headset and swears a few times to clear her head, then lowers the soundproofing again so that she doesn't feel as boxed-in.

Okay. She should stop wasting time thinking of new ways of saying "motherfucker" and start working towards not getting blown up instead.

The first three packets take her two hours. Olivia begins to wonder if "explode" means an epic drive failure beyond salvation or if there's a blast radius in her near future. Sam would be annoyed with her if she ended up as a wet smear on the ceiling of a beige data centre.

But in the process of finding those three packets she's learned the rhythm of her machine, the quirks of how information is broken up and sorted and stored. The little tricks to circumvent the white noise of general data and to get to the messy vivid tangle at the heart of things. The next ten packets only take her an hour to find and piece together.

The final one, as if to remind her that getting cocky is a good way to wind up getting dead, takes her forty-five minutes. Still, fifteen minutes to stitch together the data into a string of numbers and letters is pretty good time management, in Olivia's opinion.

The dialog box pops up on her screen again as she completes the sequence.

Congratulations. You're not useless. I'll be in contact again tomorrow.

Olivia flops back into her chair, her heart racing and her hands shaking and her eyes aching from forgetting to blink. She can't stop grinning.

25

The cafeteria is usually quiet. Everyone's too worn out to make much small talk, and that suits Olivia fine. These days she's too sad to know what to say to people who aren't Sam, most of the time.

But when she goes for dinner after her race against the clock, the room's buzzing with conversation.

'What's everyone excited about?' she asks the girl in front of her in the line. She used to be in the same dorm as Olivia and Sam, but got transferred to another department a while back. Ellie, Olivia thinks her name is.

'It was all over the radio this afternoon, you didn't hear?'

'I'm in one of the offices now,' Olivia tells her. 'We mostly don't have music on, in case our phone rings.' *Also I was trying to stop my computer exploding*, she doesn't add.

'Oh. Well, you know the Baker trial, that guy who ripped off all those people's investment portfolios and stuff?'

'Yeah.' Everyone's heard about that. Olivia remembers hearing her father rant about the scandal when it first broke.

'Well, one of the guys he cheated gave one of those victim impact statements to the court today. His wife got sick and they didn't have any money left for treatment, and she died.'

Olivia raises her eyebrows. 'And everyone's talking about that? I mean, not to paint everyone as a sociopath with a single stroke or anything, but the death of a random person's not exactly usual lunchroom gossip around here.'

'No, no, it's not that,' Ellie confirms, waving a hand as if the idea needs to be physically dismissed from the air between them.

A bracelet of old green-brown bruises rings one of her thin wrists, the kind that happen when someone bigger and stronger grabs the arm and squeezes hard. 'The victim guy, he had one of those voltage switcher adaptor things, you know, like you use if you've got a toaster that needs fifty volts but your wall outlet's 125? It changes the charge?'

'Sure, I guess,' Olivia says with a shrug.

'He had one plugged into his fucking wrist ports while he talked. It totally messed with everyone in the room who was ported. Some of the news stations are saying it doubled the normal feedback output. I doubt it was doubling – one adaptor wouldn't do that – but it was strong enough that everyone in the room who was ported wound up in tears from the osmotic pressure.'

'He could transfer that much emotion without a direct physical connection? Really?' Olivia feels a swoop of fear in her stomach, worry for Sam. What if someone used that same technique to do something horrible to everyone with ports? She'd have no way to protect Sam from that.

'Baker stood up and shouted that he was guilty after three minutes of it,' Ellie says, nodding. 'But get this, the victim impact guy? He completely blasted his heart out. Dropped dead right on the courtroom stand.'

Olivia is relieved for half a second, because if it's fatal that means nobody's gonna do it to themselves to hurt someone else randomly. But the relief ices over and turns heavy in her gut as she realises that this means that anyone who really wants to do it is going to go out and grab somebody ported, and hook *them* up to the adaptor instead.

'Fuck,' she says with feeling. Ellie nods.

'I know, right? As if there isn't already enough shit for us worker drones to wade through.' She sighs and shakes her head. 'They just keep piling it on.'

26

Why is a raven like a writing desk?
   Soubrette: They're both full of bird viscera.
   Soubrette: Also, good morning.
   Good morning.
   You recently expressed an interest in setting up grey nodes within the servers of local solar and nuclear stations.
   Soubrette: You were doing better when you were asking a riddle. Making statements leads to a conversation that's mostly me going 'yes?' And considering how that went for me yesterday, I'd rather we find a different pattern.
   I've put the file with the necessary steps on your system. Some signal range issues are slowing down the process of contacting Red Rabbit. It'll take me a few more days. That gives you more than enough time to set up the nodes.
   Soubrette: Is that what I owe you, as payment for your help?
   Contrary to rumour, I don't keep a ledger of checks and balances. I find that a facile concept.
   I want to be treated as I've treated others, but that's what most people want.
   Soubrette: Are you sure you want that? You put me through some seriously game-show bullshit yesterday, don't forget. If I were you I'd be hoping nobody ever treated me like that in return.
   You had fun.
   Soubrette: That's not
   Soubrette: That's not the point!

27

That evening she sits on the end of Sam's bed, near his feet. Her own legs are drawn up to her chest, her chin resting on her forearms, crossed atop her knees.

'Sam?'

He's lying very, very still, a cloth covering his eyes against the light of the bare bulb in the ceiling. His 'hm?' of acknowledgement is faint.

'Why is a raven like a writing desk?'

'Both have inky quills.'

'Oh. Cool.' Olivia nods thoughtfully, even though Sam can't see it.

'Why?'

'Someone asked me today, that's all. I answered that they're both full of bird viscera.'

Sam gives the smallest, quietest laugh Olivia has ever heard. 'Creep.'

'Do you want me to read to you?'

'Not this time.'

She doesn't say anything for a few minutes, and then: 'Sam, I don't want to stay here. You're getting hurt.'

'Don't start with that again. I don't have the energy for this.'

'That's half the problem. You're wearing yourself out. Would you be doing this much if it was just you, and not both of us? Are you enduring *whatever* because you think you have to, for my sake?'

He doesn't say a word. He doesn't move, apart from the steady rise and fall of his breathing. Olivia could kill the whole world with nothing but the fire of how angry she is. All she wants is for Sam to be safe and happy and not in pain. It doesn't seem such an outrageous wish.

'I'm not your babysitter,' she says, her voice slow and deliberate. 'And *you aren't mine*. We're in this together. And I don't want to be here anymore, where kids get hurt because we don't have any power to fight back with, where you're working yourself sick.'

'This isn't an especially bad factory,' Sam tells her quietly, not moving to uncover his eyes. 'I've seen much worse. We're okay.'

Because he can't see her, Olivia doesn't worry about stopping her tears from falling. She wipes at her cheeks with the heel of her hand and draws in a deep breath, calming herself enough that her voice will sound even when she speaks.

'No. I can't watch you do this to yourself anymore. I'm... I think I might be on my way to finding somewhere else we can go, or at least to somebody who can help us. If I'm right, will you come with me?'

Sam pulls the cloth off and props himself up on his elbows, looking at her sharply. His face is pale, his eyes bright.

'I would go with you anywhere,' he tells her simply, like it's the most obvious thing in the world. 'I had the strength to say goodbye once, and you didn't let me. I don't have nearly enough courage to do it a second time. You're stuck with me now.'

Olivia has to wipe her cheeks again. She gives him a crooked smile, then a snuffly laugh. 'Okay. Good. You're stuck with me, too.'

She gently takes the cloth from his hand and pushes his shoulders back down, until he's lying with his head on the pillow again. She replaces the cloth in its earlier position.

'You get some rest, and I'll be here when you're better.'

28

You're nimble with your coding.

Soubrette: Thanks. I'm not used to getting into systems like this

Soubrette: So I'm being extra careful with what I brush against

RedRabbit has invited you into secure chat.

WARNING Do not accept secure chats from people you don't know. Do not accept secure chats while ported to your machine.

RedRabbit: !

Soubrette: !

RedRabbit: !!

Soubrette: !!!!!!!!!!!!!!!!

RedRabbit: should have known id never get rid of you

Soubrette: Don't get cranky at me for your lack of foresight.

RedRabbit: whats happening

RedRabbit: the ones who came to tell me didnt know much

How's Arachne?

Soubrette: Does the concept of 'private chat' just not register with you?

RedRabbit: good

RedRabbit: her + her bros were going on a hunt when i left

RedRabbit: no idea what they expect to find this time of year thats edible

RedRabbit: she said to say thanks

Tell her it was my pleasure.

RedRabbit: yeah ok

RedRabbit: we need a better message system

RedRabbit: that drive eats petrol like hell

You could always move closer than the pulses.

RedRabbit: fuck off

Olivia only realises how broadly she's smiling when her mouth starts to hurt.

RedRabbit: ok anyway

RedRabbit: whats happening

Soubrette: I'm working at a factory but it's bad. I need somewhere else where Sam and I can go instead.

Soubrette: And I wanted to find you again.

RedRabbit: i live outside the city now

RedRabbit: its not easy but compared to a factory its heaven

RedRabbit: do you want to come with me

Soubrette: Yes.

Olivia types and sends the reply before she's fully registered the question. She doesn't have to think about pros and cons. Even if she did, she'd want to go no matter how reckless the choice might be from a cost/benefit viewpoint. Some things are simpler than logic.

RedRabbit: send me the address i can be there today

Soubrette: Thank you.

RedRabbit: hey i owe you one from back then

RedRabbit: no need to thank me

Soubrette: No that's gross.

Soubrette: You don't owe me anything.

Soubrette: You never did.

RedRabbit: whatever give me address

29

They arrange to meet in the loading dock in a few hours' time. Olivia can't concentrate on anything once the plans are made. She doesn't try to hack again. She's certain she'll make a dumb mistake and screw everything up. She's a bundle of nerves.

When it gets closer to the agreed time, Olivia shuts down her terminal and goes to the factory floor level to find Sam. She finally finds him in the tiny, dingy kitchenette, standing beside the fridge with his forehead against the quietly humming enamel.

He starts reflexively at the sound of someone entering the room, and she can tell from his posture that he's been caught in here before and yelled at for it. When Sam sees that it's her, his shoulders slump in relief and he gives her a nod.

'Hi.'

'Hey. I've found us somewhere else to go. Come on, let's get our stuff.'

Sam raises his eyebrows. 'Now?'

'Would you rather stay to the end of your shift?'

'Well, when you put it that way.' He follows her to their dorm.

There isn't much to collect. They always keep their money – what little they've managed to save – on them. There's nowhere safe enough to stash it, so it's always in their pockets. All they have in the dormitory is a small bundle of clothes and their readers, which are battered old second-hand models that nobody has bothered to steal from them.

On their way from the dorm to the loading dock, they pass Ellie in the hallway.

'Here,' Olivia says to her, handing over her keypass to the office level. 'Take over being me. Nobody's going to notice, trust me. There's a hundred of us up there, and I never got to know anyone. You'd know as well as I do that they never check ID here.'

'Where are you going?' Ellie asks, taking the offered keypass.

'Away.' Olivia shrugs. 'Don't know yet. Somewhere else.'

The loading dock is as empty at this hour of the day as it is on the nights when they've come out to run. Hardly anyone tries to transport anything except in the most off-peak of times; there's no point with traffic the way it is.

'Still taller than everyone else, I see.'

Hannah's on the other side of the perimeter fence. A scar sweeps down from the outer corner of her eye to bite into the meat of her cheek, like the curve of a sickle blade. Apart from that addition, her face is just as Olivia remembers it.

She's real. She's safe. She's here.

'Stand back for a second,' Hannah says, interrupting Olivia's slightly dazed happy staring. Olivia does as instructed, taking a few steps back along with Sam. Hannah takes a running jump at the fence between them. Her fingers and the toes of her boots find purchase, her hands grab the wire. She pulls herself up and over the razor coils at the top, like a child on a climbing frame.

She drops down and lands near them, her own smile sharp and feral.

She's wearing the flimsy polyester uniform shirt issued to all workers in the factories. Olivia thinks it's meant to be a disguise, to make Hannah blend in with the neighbourhood, but it doesn't work at all. On Hannah it looks like a costume, a borrowed raiment that's *on* her but not *of* her. For Olivia and the other factory kids, the uniform becomes so much a part of them, a part of the grind, that it's as if it has seeped into their skin.

'That outfit is about as convincing as a fake moustache on a twelve-year-old who's trying to get into a strip club,' Olivia says to the girl she's missed so badly.

'I thought about method acting on the assembly line for a few hours, but then I thought, why not just stick ports in both my eyeballs and jack my brain full of a monotone hum of electric feedback instead, because it'd be less shitty and boring,' Hannah retorts.

'At least tie your hair back. We have to wear ours in buns, like this.' Olivia turns, pointing at the plaited coil at the nape of her neck. Hannah pulls an elastic band out of the pocket of her battered canvas pants – which, Olivia notes, don't even pay lip service to the idea of matching uniform regulations – and knots her long hair into a messy bundle.

Hannah's hair is the most dramatic change to how she looks, even more than the scar. The scruff she wore when Olivia first met her has grown out into a long, loose fall of light brown waves, streaked with premature grey.

'You are so bad at this,' Olivia says, oddly impressed by Hannah's inability to dress as someone downtrodden.

'Sorry your majesty.' Hannah rolls her eyes. 'Can we blow this joint? I want to get home before dawn if we can. We have to walk a lot of it; I wanted to save fuel.'

Olivia's stomach drops, like she's gone down a dozen storeys in a high-speed elevator. This is real. Hannah's here. It's over.

They climb the fence – Olivia and Sam managing it somewhat less gracefully than Hannah – and set off, blending into the sparse crowd of other uniformed kids who are out and about at this time of day for whatever reason.

Olivia considers the size of the factory zone, and how many tens of thousands, maybe hundreds of thousands, of people must live and work in the area. For there to be only this light scatter of pedestrians visible, it must mean that the vast majority of the local population is shut away and working at that very moment. Add up all the small miseries endured by each person, and the sum total is a bigger amount of unhappiness than Olivia wants to ever have to think about.

She'll carry her factory months with her forever, she's sure.

She hopes that the memory of how awful they've been will make her a more compassionate, kinder person. Right now mostly they've made her tired and sad.

'I forgot how horrible it is here,' Hannah remarks, making a face. 'Metal and cement, metal and cement. How do you cope without anything green?'

'We look forlorn,' Sam answers immediately, in his habitual flat tones. The reply takes Olivia a second to process, and then she groans.

'No. No puns. I can't handle puns right now.'

Hannah looks at Sam, like she's only just noticed him there. 'Did you hear about the guy whose whole left side was cut off?' she asks him.

Sam shakes his head.

'He's all right now,' Hannah finishes. Sam grins delightedly as Olivia winces.

'No. No. Stop. Both of you. No more of this.'

'What's the problem with shoplifters?' Sam asks.

'What?'

'They take things literally.'

'If you keep this up I'm going back to the factory.'

'I'm reading a book about anti-gravity. It's impossible to put down.'

'I wondered why the baseball was getting bigger. Then it hit me.'

'I hate you both. I hate you both *so much*,' Olivia wails.

30

After a while, they feel the low air quality with every breath. Olivia's got a headache and her throat hurts. They buy bandanas from a stall and soak them in the plastic tub provided. The water has a faintly herbal smell to it, which helps soothe Olivia's headache. Tying the cloths across their mouths and noses stops the worst of the fumes from getting into their systems.

Their voices are muffled this way, though, so for a while they don't talk much. It's a companionable quiet, all of them in good moods.

The factories give way to high-density housing. What little scent gets through to Olivia through the cloth shifts from the chemical stink of industry to the fecund, organic smells of too many people living too close together without enough waste disposal.

That neighbourhood thins out into smaller apartment buildings, and then individual houses, which gradually go from being tiny and crowded to more spaced apart and much, much bigger. They're still considerably smaller than the house where Olivia grew up.

As the day wears on, the ratio of occupied houses to abandoned ones tips in favour of vacancies, and Olivia can't help the shiver up her back. They're in the outskirts now, right on the edge of the city. They're about to leave the only official site of civilisation for thousands of miles in every direction.

'Don't turn your readers on anymore,' Hannah tells them, pulling her bandana down to rest around her neck. Olivia and

Sam copy her action, and the three of them are properly face-to-face again. 'We'll be hitting the margin soon.'

'The pulses?' Sam guesses. Hannah nods.

'Yep. There's no way to predict them, and anything that's turned on when they hit gets completely fried. You're stuck with analogue everything, out here.'

As she speaks, Hannah plays with a necklace she's wearing under the damp bandana. It's a thin silver chain, oxidized to a dark patina over time. A single white tooth hangs from it, like a pendant.

The tooth is triangular, sharp as a fang, curved a fraction too much to the left to be symmetrical. It's far too big to be a human tooth, or the tooth of any animal that Olivia can imagine Hannah having an opportunity to fight.

'It's from a shark,' Hannah answers Olivia's unasked question as the three of them walk on. 'I found it at the market a while back and it… I like thinking about the ocean. I remember you talking about it, and I liked remembering that.'

'Pliny the Elder thought shark teeth fell from the sky during solar eclipses. Like rain, or hail,' Sam says. 'He wrote the very first encyclopaedia. The first thing we would recognise as being an encyclopaedia, with indexing and references and all of that stuff.'

'Sam loves anything from Ancient Greece and Rome,' Olivia tells Hannah.

'Sounds like a shitty encyclopaedia, then, if it had "facts" like that,' Hannah observes.

'It has information on animals like phoenixes and cynocephali – humans with dog heads – and it has recipes and information about food preparation, too. Pliny the Elder died in the volcanic eruption that destroyed Pompeii,' replies Sam.

'Okay, I take it back, that sounds like an *awesome* encyclopaedia. I'm gonna hunt down a copy for the library at the complex.'

'Graduated to a whole library now, huh?' Olivia asks with a

grin, remembering Hannah's much-loved stack of paperbacks.

'I'm a bowerbird. Or is it a magpie? The one that can't stop collecting shiny objects. I never met a book I didn't want to hoard.'

'The complex?' Sam asks.

'It's a couple of old apartment blocks, built around a central courtyard, with a gate at the front. Nothing too fancy, but it's done well for all of us there. People move in and out, but I've been there a while now, and so have a few others. I think you'll like it. We've got okay water filtration, and we've cleared the neighbourhood around it well enough that there's not much fire risk.'

She pauses, squinting at the smog-hazy sky. 'I don't think we'll make it to the car early enough to drive tonight, though. I don't want to be on foot when evening hits. We'll bunk down out here and set off again tomorrow.'

'Can we stop for a second?' Olivia asks. 'Before we hit the margin? If we're not in so much of a hurry anymore, I want to grab a minute on a terminal before we go out of range.'

'Okay, sure,' Hannah agrees with a shrug.

They find a public station and buy a few packets of food. In the corner is a table scattered with a few dingy paperbacks, which surprises Olivia – she's never seen a store sell hard-copy books out in the open before. She guesses that this close to the margin, it's much harder to encourage people to use readers instead, so that their habits can be monitored.

Hannah and Sam browse the selection of titles while Olivia opens a command window and fiddles in the program files until she's comfortable that she's dodging the more obnoxious security systems in place.

Soubrette: Are you there?

Naturally.

Soubrette: I don't know why I thought I even had to ask.

Soubrette: You'll have to tell me how you do that one day.

Soubrette: Anyway.

Soubrette: I'm about to go out past the margin.

Soubrette: It might be a while until I'm back in range.

Soubrette: I wanted to say thank you.

In that case, thank you in return for the work you did on the nodes.

Soubrette: It's too bad that we both hate the idea of owing favours.

Soubrette: We could argue about who owes who.

Soubrette: Okay, I gotta go.

Soubrette: Thank you, Carabosse.

I hope things go well for you, until the next time we talk, Olivia.

She never gave her real name in any of her chats, but she's not remotely surprised that her mysterious mentor knows it. She'll have to ask the girl that Carabosse and Hannah mentioned – Arachne, Olivia thinks it was – about who Carabosse is. Two can play at information-digging.

When she rejoins Hannah and Sam by the book table, Hannah's counting coins from a pouch onto her palm.

'Buying a book?'

'Yeah, that one,' Hannah nods at one of the paperbacks. It's a copy of *The General Theory of Employment, Interest and Money* by John Maynard Keynes, of all things.

'I actually really love this stuff,' Hannah confesses, sounding sheepish. She's speaking to Sam and doesn't look at Olivia.

'There was a bunch of... I wound up with a reader full of that kind of shit, a while ago. I was surprised by how into it I got.'

Olivia imagines Hannah creeping back into the little cement room on the same night they'd left it. Maybe a few nights later. Were the bodies still there? Was there blood on the ground, stains that were all that remained of the people she'd known, the maskers she'd thrown in with?

She wonders what Hannah went back for in particular. Her mask? The stack of books? Whatever the main objective had been, Olivia's glad that Hannah took the reader as well. It makes Olivia feel less of a creepy weirdo over how often she's thought of Hannah since those days. It's not nearly so messed up that she did, if Hannah was thinking about her as well.

31

In the late afternoon, they reach the desolate bulk of a shopping centre, squat and grey and long-discarded among the empty roads and houses. Hannah clambers easily through a smashed-in window on the eastern side, then waits for them to manoeuvre after her.

'There are some stores that're barely touched. Fewer, as the years go on,' she tells them. 'But I still prefer it here to the houses. It doesn't feel so much like intrusion when you go through the things here.'

'The owners of the stuff in the houses aren't coming back for any of it,' Sam points out.

Hannah shrugs. 'I prefer it here. Stores were designed for strangers. It's not so much like a tomb.'

'Are there still houses? Unraided, sitting just as they were when the evacuations happened?' Olivia asks.

'Oh, yeah.' Hannah nods. 'You'd be surprised at how many there are, hiding out there in the sprawl. They're like... like Donkeyskin, from that old fairy tale? They're so boring and ugly and unkempt that nobody notices, not even the really good raiders.'

Olivia's left momentarily speechless by the fact that Hannah knows the same obscure story that Olivia herself loves so much, that the same key element of it stood out for them both.

'You notice them,' Sam notes.

'I don't go in, though. They're... not nice. I don't like being in them. They're sad.'

Nice. Sad. Clumsy, inarticulate words when usually Hannah

has such a sharp and clever tongue. Hannah's loss for words tells Olivia everything.

'We'll leave them be, then,' she says. Gratitude flits across Hannah's face for a moment.

'We can see if they have any of those giant leather recliner chairs anywhere in the stores here,' Hannah says a few seconds later, her usual swagger returning. 'I've always wanted to sleep in one of those.'

They sleep on thick feather quilts that smell musty from being folded up on display shelves for so many years. Even with the plush thickness of the coverlet under her, Olivia can feel the flat, hard floor beneath. It's no more uncomfortable than the unforgiving wire springs of the factory bunk-beds with their worn foam mattresses, so it doesn't take Olivia long to fall asleep. All the walking tired them out.

Waking up is strange, though. The thin overlay between her and the ground reminds her of the bedroll in the little cement room. But that was a long time ago, now, and this time when she wakes it's to the sight of Sam and Hannah nearby, both of them sleeping.

Olivia is sore but invigorated, equal parts excited and nervous to see what lies ahead. She eats a few mouthfuls of the food they bought yesterday and then undoes her hair, combing it out with her fingers before she rebraids it.

'It grew back, I see.'

Olivia turns at Hannah's voice, and nods. 'Good morning.'

'If you say so,' Hannah mutters, scratching her head and yawning. 'It's nearly as long as it was when we cut it off.'

'I kept it short for a long time, after. My mother hated it. She said it didn't flatter my face. I think that's why I got so stubborn about it, because she made it such a big deal. I only started growing it again because Sam likes to fiddle with it while he's thinking.'

'That why you wear glasses, too? To bug your mother?'

Olivia shrugs. 'Not completely. I like having them on. They feel like a mask. The prescription's old now, though. I'm sure the factory work screwed up my vision a lot faster than reading late at night ever did, but I haven't had a new pair for a while now, so I get headaches a bit.'

'That sucks. The only thing we've got at the complex that might help are a couple of old magnifying glasses, for people to use for books and stuff if their eyesight's bad.'

'Oh, cool. That'll be useful.'

'We should get going soon. Get back to the car to beat the midday sun,' Hannah notes. She nudges Sam's side with her toe. 'Wake up, Sleeping Beauty.'

Sam makes a disgruntled noise and pulls his blanket over his head. 'Sleeping Beauty refuses.'

'Sleeping Beauty has absolutely no agency whatsoever in her narrative,' Olivia tells him cheerfully, pulling the blanket away. 'So she can't refuse.'

'I'm a postmodern interpretation,' Sam grumbles, but he gets up and helps them pack their things.

They reach Hannah's car a few hours later. It's dusty and dented enough that it blends with the ever-present scatter of abandoned ones left on the roads. Opening the doors and climbing inside feels weird, and it isn't even a real wreck, so Olivia starts to understand why Hannah didn't want to go inside any of the houses. Disturbing the tableau would be like digging up a grave just to see what was inside.

It's a solid, old-fashioned model. Olivia doesn't know a thing about cars; she only rode in them when her parents insisted, always preferring trains if there was a choice. Hannah's car is high and slightly boxy, with a big storage space at the back. Several large plastic bottles sit in this back area, under a heatproof blanket, and they give the interior a sharp petrol stink.

Hannah's a surprisingly careful driver, so the ride is smooth, almost pleasant. The streets of houses and stores seem less desolate from inside the car, the emptiness less obvious.

'All the furniture's gone from the empty apartments at the complex,' Hannah tells them. 'So you don't have to worry about it feeling like this when you go inside any of them. Everything's long gone. All they need is an ordinary spring clean and they're fresh again. I've been sharing with some of the other single tenants, Esperanza mostly, but now that you two are coming along too, it's probably best if we clean up one of the spares, and the three of us take that.'

'Or...' she adds after a moment, her eyes fixed on the road. 'I guess you two can have one to yourselves. If you want that.'

'No, you're good. I like you,' Sam replies before Olivia has a chance to answer.

'You can have your own room,' Olivia enthuses to Sam. 'You can have a desk for drawing, and shelves and baskets for your books and gadgets, and-'

'I don't want my own room. Not to sleep in,' Sam tells her flatly.

Olivia's surprised by that. They kept close on cold nights in the factory, yes, but things weren't going to be bad like that from now on. Things weren't going to be frightening like that. And there had been a lot of nights where Sam couldn't stand to have anyone near him and where even the sounds of breathing had made him flinch.

'Well, we'll see,' she answers, trying to be diplomatic. He'll change his mind. He just doesn't realise the situation properly yet.

'You're doing it again,' Sam says. It's observational, rather than irritated, so Olivia decides to drop the subject for the time being.

32

Olivia sleeps for a while, lulled by the motion of the car, so when they reach the complex her first impressions of it are filtered through a sluggish, cotton-wool brain. The buildings are old, a few long cracks crazing up the brickwork of the walls. It makes her remember that no security is permanent, no structure so sturdy that time won't eventually pull it down.

That's an ominous note to begin on, but she soon pushes it aside and takes in the careful way that any panes of broken glass in the apartment windows have been replaced with wooden shutters. The shutters are painted in bright block colours or decorative patterns, to easily let light in or keep out rain and cold.

A girl about Olivia's age is standing by the high gates as Hannah drives up. She has the kind of face that Olivia thinks of as "weathered", the sort people get if they have a lot of harsh wind and sun in their days. Her hair is a brittle pale blonde, her skin tanned dark and mottled with freckles that are darker still.

The short hem of her faded sundress leaves most of her legs bare, revealing a wide burn scar winding crookedly from one ankle up past where the skirt covers her thigh.

'How did the hunt go?' Hannah asks, opening her door and climbing down. She'll show these two around before she parks the car near the fuel house down the block.

The girl shrugs. 'It went okay. Nothing living, but we found a carton of baked beans. None of the cans are even dented.'

Hannah whistles appreciatively. '*Nice*. This is Olivia and

Sam. Olivia and Sam, Ariette. She and her brothers are the ones that brought the message about you needing help.'

'Hi.' Olivia raises one hand in a tentative wave. 'Carabosse called you Arachne?'

Ariette gives a derisive snort. 'Fuck, those names sound dumb as shit said out loud. Yeah, that's me.'

'Thanks for bringing the message.'

Another shrug from Ariette, this one radiating disinterest even more obviously than the first. 'It was worth my while. I got told about this place in exchange for bringing the news. My brothers and I had been angling to get out of the city for a while, but there's no point in leaving if you don't have any idea where to go.'

'I'm tired and I want a bath,' Hannah interrupts. 'Enough chit-chat.'

She leads them through the gate and through the gap between two of the high brick walls. Beyond that, the space widens out into a large central courtyard. Balconies overlook the area from the apartments above, and there's a sense of peace, of *safety*, that's unlike anywhere Olivia has ever been.

When Olivia looks at Hannah, she's watching Olivia's expression with a small satisfied smile. 'Yeah, it's pretty good, isn't it?' she agrees. 'Now let's go find where we can bed you two, until we get a new place set up for all of us.'

33

They start work on their new home the next day, scrubbing every surface, replacing broken doors and windows. When it's ready for them to move in, Hannah takes them down the street to the store houses – two ordinary suburban homes that have been cleaned out of their previous contents and filled with things that aren't kept at the complex itself.

There's fuel for the car, stored here as a safety precaution. It looks a huge amount to Olivia, but she remembers what Hannah said about how quickly it depletes.

There also seems to be the entire contents of a high-school science supplies closet, shoved into boxes and stored in a kitchen pantry. Large rolled-up charts of the periodic table, a plastic dummy of a human torso with removable organs, and a dozen small specimens.

'We might have more room someday, for a bigger library,' Hannah answers when Olivia queries the purpose of keeping these supplies. 'Or there might be enough outliers to start a school, who knows? They aren't hurting anyone.'

She sounds defensive, and Olivia's reminded suddenly of Sam's orthographic projection drawings. Once upon a time, those drawings had made Olivia wonder if, in a very different world, Sam might have grown up to be an architect. Now she wonders about Hannah, remembers how Hannah demanded that Olivia give reading fiction a proper try. Maybe in that very different world, Hannah could have been a teacher.

To decorate their new home, Olivia borrows one of the smaller school displays. A conch shell, a perfect pink spiral.

The smooth texture of it is comforting in her palm. She wonders if this is how other people feel when they touch rosaries or prayer stones. Soothed by the fact of an object's existence.

She likes the perfect fractal of its shape, and she likes how it makes her think of *Lord of the Flies*, how the characters in that story decided that the conch shell meant a right to speak and to be heard. These days, Olivia's voice is slowly growing back.

34

Cooking is like hacking, but with water and flour instead of encryptions and files. Olivia has the same sense of accomplishment in both, the creation of something that didn't exist before, of manipulating the elements around her until they build exactly what she wants.

For a long, long time, she's eaten to stop hunger, and that's all. That's all either of them did at the factory. Before that, Sam's relationship with food had been governed by the souvlaki place; food was work, a way to earn a wage to stay alive. Olivia's appetite had been curbed by having to share meals with her parents.

She has a more complicated feeling when she thinks about her parents now, than she ever did when she lived with them, but that new sense of nuance doesn't change the way her memories feel, the knot in her stomach that stopped her enjoying their dinners and breakfasts together.

Neither Olivia nor Sam has ever had the opportunity to associate food with *nourishment* before, not the way that characters in stories so often do. But it starts to make sense to them, as Hannah teaches them little tricks and they learn how to create meals that taste really good.

Of the three of them, Sam is the one who loves cooking the most. It starts one evening, not long after they've moved in, while Olivia's preparing vegetables for their meal. He picks up the Romanesco broccoli off the chopping board, turning it this way and that in his hand.

'This has a recursive helical arrangement of cones. We might as well be eating a perfect computer-generated concept. A graphed statistic grown out of the earth.'

'Full of vitamins, too,' she replies. 'Pick up a knife and start chopping.'

And with that, Ancient Greece and the properties of three-dimensional shapes are joined by a third major interest in Sam's repertoire.

'We should get some ferns,' he suggests to Hannah on the following afternoon. 'A few small pots. Ferns are natural fractals, like the broccoli. Each leaf is a miniature replication of their structure as a whole. Each fern plant is both male and female, possessing within itself all the things it needs to create more ferns, which in turn are able to do the same. Replication upon replication. Fern spores are the perfect algorithm. A formula, ready and waiting to be graphed across the world, the line never breaking no matter how far it is extrapolated.'

Hannah, whose life has contained things much, much stranger than a boy who likes formulas and patterns, shrugs one shoulder. 'Sure, I'll ask around about seeds. But you're watering them.'

35

The courtyard in the centre of the complex is partially paved in one corner, a remnant of what it looked like before the evacuations.

Between the carefully irregular, faux-rustic stones that were once laid evenly over the ground, wild vines and flowers have sprung up. Dagger-like sharp weeds and grasses are a brilliant green against the mica-flecked grey of the granite paving.

Most of the earth in the open space has been exposed and turned, fed with mulch and fertiliser and planted with rows of vegetables and fruits. Every balcony overhanging the courtyard is festooned with pots of herbs and smaller crops, tomato plants and citrus trees growing in buckets and salvaged ceramic fixtures. The smell is a riot of life, a scent that's nothing like the ocean but somehow reminds Olivia of being by the sea. This is the smell of the world when it's pulsing, alive, transforming.

Garlands of paper lights decorate some of the balcony railings, fitted with tiny candles and lit on still evenings. The flames make the colours of their paper bulbs flicker and dance, a swarm of rainbow baubles in the dark.

On those nights, Hannah, Sam, Olivia and everyone else not busy with their work all gather in the courtyard, sitting carefully among the crops as they talk and eat their dinners and laugh together. The five storeys of the apartments stretch up like castle walls around them, decorated with the paper lights and their ever-shifting candle glow.

Their apartment is only a little bigger, in total, than Olivia's old bedroom and en-suite. She boggles at this fact when it occurs to her, because she has no idea how she ever managed to fill such a space, to make it feel like it all belonged to her. Sometimes she feels as if they'll never occupy all of the apartment. They'll never fill it up with so much of themselves that it'll be truly theirs.

Even with more space than they know what to do with, Olivia and Sam sleep curled together. He was right about that after all. She's glad that he was, glad that he's there next to her in the night. Just in case she needs to protect him, or he needs to protect her. It only takes a few weeks before Hannah joins them. The bed is big enough for three.

36

Ariette's brothers are Jesse and Eric. Olivia doesn't know if the three of them really are related, or if they're a put-together family like Olivia, Sam and Hannah are. It doesn't matter one way or the other, so she doesn't ask.

Eric and Jesse have burns, like Ariette. Eric doesn't have use of his left hand because of the damage to it, and one of Jesse's ears and part of his cheek, neck, and shoulder are blurred and sore-looking from the scars.

Jesse, the most talkative of the three, tells Olivia that when they were very young, the farm they lived on was declared reclaimed government property. When their parents refused to vacate, the farm burned, along with a huge swathe of the land surrounding it.

There's no way to prove the city played any part in this destruction, of course. But the triplets have always been certain of where to lay the blame for the countless lives lost, the need to rebuild from scratch.

'That's why Ariette got into the online stuff, became Arachne,' Jesse explains. 'The other hackers used to tell her off for being too reckless, for breaking into high-security systems that could track her down if she did too much damage or lingered too long. She didn't care. So long as she could make life as hard as possible for as many of those fuckers as she could, she didn't care how dangerous people said it was.'

'Why'd you leave, then?'

'Because Eric and I knew it couldn't last,' Jesse answers.

'When she got into it, really into it, we knew that she wouldn't stop on her own until she destroyed herself. She needed us to pull her back.'

Olivia can't imagine ever feeling like Jesse says Ariette did, but she accepts the answer. Nobody out in this part of the world winds up here by living a calm, easily understood life. All Olivia can do is accept people the way they are.

37

Most of the outliers are young, the numbers dropping off to almost none by the age of forty or so. There's not exactly a retirement plan for their kind of life. Olivia doesn't care about that – she'd rather be happy for fifteen years than wretched for thirty, if her future is forced into a choice between the two – but she gets frustrated by how it means she has to hang around with a whole bunch of immature jerks sometimes.

Nobody at the complex is like that, thank goodness, but she notices a few at the bonfires and markets that they go to. The small pack of sharp-eyed, sharp-tongued kids reminds Olivia of the bullies at her school, from a life so far removed from this one that it makes her want to laugh. Even here, in the ruins of the world, some people can't help being terrible.

Hannah notices them, too. They laugh at her behind their hands, casting their gazes up and down her form at moments when they're sure she'll notice. They sneer at her clothes, the worn brown leather coat she wears on cooler days and the shark tooth on its chain and her black boots.

Those looks don't seem to bother Hannah, but when they whisper and laugh at the grey in her hair she blushes and looks away, all her vim and bravado deflated.

'They don't matter,' Olivia tells her on the way home, but the words are empty. After all, Hannah's still a kid, too, no matter what world exists around them.

It's not a complete surprise to Olivia when, a few days later,

Hannah dyes her hair rich and red, like coppery earth, covering the grey.

The pretty, lustrous shade doesn't help, of course. Olivia could have predicted that, if she'd thought about it. Once you're marked as a target, almost nothing you do will shake a bully loose.

The nasty kids whisper "Hannah uses henna" whenever she's in earshot. It's a harmless accusation on the surface, but Olivia can hear the venom underneath. For those kids, this is somehow proof that Hannah is deficient and different and strange.

As if those things aren't true about all of them. As if that isn't the very thing that makes them who they are.

On the day before the next market gathering, Ariette dyes her brittle locks to a deep and vivid blue. The colour is uneven, darker in some places than other, and the effect reminds Olivia of the ocean on clear days, deeper currents and shallow sections each throwing up their own particular shade.

Ariette bares her small, even teeth with a vicious smile. 'Let them try to find a rhyme for 'woad and indigo leaves'.' It sounds like a challenge, cold and deadly.

Jesse and Eric show up in the courtyard a few hours later, hair in brilliant shades of crimson and green respectively. Esperanza's is a vivid mustard yellow.

'Shit,' Sam says quietly, so only Olivia can hear. 'I want to join in. It's to support Hannah. I love Hannah. But having a colour like that would...' He trails off, hands fluttering anxiously.

Olivia nods, understanding. Wearing bright, intense shades makes Sam feel sick and dizzy.

'We'll go black and white, instead,' she tells him. Olivia's happier with that idea. She loves colours, would fill the whole world with colours if she could, paint it all, but she never feels very colourful herself. She feels like she's meant to be monochrome.

By evening they're done, Sam's hair bleached to a blonde that's almost white, and Olivia's darkened to a blue-black.

At the market the next day, all of them together in their hues, they are untouchable. No whispers or taunts could ever hurt them like this.

38

Since they all share the one bedroom for sleeping, and spend so much of their time in the kitchen, Hannah, Sam and Olivia decide to convert the extra bedroom of their apartment into a pantry.

They devote an entire bookshelf in this new space to the jams they make, strawberry and grape and blueberry and apricot. Some of the food in their pantry is salvage, picked up by Hannah on her runs out into the abandoned wilds: cans of beans or soup or things like that. But none of their jams come from there.

Olivia doesn't think she could be happy eating old discarded city jams, now that she's tasted the ones her own hands can make.

They make their own peanut butter every couple of weeks, or more often, because they eat it so fast. Even if they didn't, they'd have to renew it regularly. Jam lasts forever but peanut butter's got a short life.

Whenever possible, they make it in the early morning before anyone else in the complex is awake and recruits them for larger labours. Hannah shells the peanuts and roasts them in a pan, shaking them every minute or so to make sure they don't burn on one side. Sam sometimes laughs aloud at this step, because the movement makes the peanuts jump into the air like fat pale fleas.

When the nuts have cooled off, Olivia plugs the food processor into the generator and puts the peanuts inside along with a little oil. Sam's the one to turn on the processor, and Olivia and Hannah always grin at how pleased he looks when the sound of the metal blades kicks in; their busy, noisy whir.

If Sam wanted to sing at the top of his lungs all night while Olivia and Hannah tried to sleep, they'd let him do it. They'd salvage some noise-cancelling headphones from an old electronics store, or make earplugs, and let Sam sing away to his heart's content. But it's not singing that Sam loves, it's this grind of the blades that smooth the peanuts into butter. So Olivia and Hannah always make sure that it's Sam who gets to press the button.

They pour the mixture into jars and put it into the fridge. By Monday morning, the butter's ready and Sam makes thick sandwiches of jam and peanut butter for them to take on their salvage runs or to the library or wherever they're going.

If Olivia had to tell somebody what "home" meant to her, she wouldn't be able to think of a better answer than the taste of those sandwiches.

39

The library is the apartment that the books are kept in. Nobody lives there, so it's two bedrooms, a living room, a kitchen and a bathroom entirely full of narrow aisles of mismatched bookshelves and haphazard stacks which stretch as high as the ceilings. It includes volumes from long-outdated encyclopaedia sets, and signed first editions stolen from museums, and paperbacks of every size and subject.

Anything from any of these books is a story eligible for the telling on those nights when everyone gathers in the courtyard.

On this particular night, the air has the chill of late autumn on it and the earth is mostly settled, the crops harvested already and laid aside for winter in the food-assigned apartment spaces.

Esperanza tells everyone about a little boy she's read about in one of the encyclopaedias. He was raised by goats for eight years. The skin of his hands and feet had hardened from years and years of cold and scars. When he walked, he did so as if he had four hooves.

When she's done, it's Hannah's turn.

'Back in the middle of the ages of the Wars, there was one called the Cold War,' she starts. Hannah likes to stand when she tells stories. Olivia, her head resting in Sam's lap as she lies stretched out on the soft earth, looks up at Hannah while she listens.

'On one side of this war were the Americans, and on the other side were the Soviets. There was fear and violence and spying and all that on both sides, naturally. Nobody's any different from their enemies when it comes to that shit.

'Almost anything that wasn't Soviet was banned in Russia, because that government thought that things made outside their Republic were decadent and corrupt. A lot of music was forbidden: jazz, pop, rock & roll.

'But you can't suppress something like that. It always bursts through. Pretty soon people realised that if they tuned their radios right, they could pick up signals from Luxembourg, a country just outside the Soviet Union. And if they picked up those signals they could record them on the big old reel-to-reel tape machines they had in those days.

'Now, okay, the thing about wars is that a lot of young people wind up soldiers, and a lot of them come from backgrounds too poor for really good educations. People like that always get to be the disposable ranks. That's one of the shittiest facts of life: the unluckiest stay the unluckiest.

'Those young soldiers couldn't read or write that well, so recording booths were set up for them in all the cities. They could speak short messages for their families back home, and the recording would be pressed onto vinyl records and posted to the soldiers' families.

'So the people who were using the big reel-to-reel tape recorders to pick up songs from other countries, they wanted to use these radio-letter machines, because that'd be a much better way to keep their music.

'They started sneaking around at night, raiding the garbage bins behind hospitals and stealing the discarded x-ray sheets. Ribs, they called them. Photographs of the insides of chests and bellies.

'They took these scavenged ribs to the recording booths for the messages home, and slipped them in where the vinyl for the record would go. Then they played their reel-to-reels into the microphone, and the sound was etched into the x-rays like scrimshaw into bone.

'The rib-records were thin and flexible enough to hide inside the sleeve of a coat. Wrapped around your arm like a bracelet, you could pass it on to someone else with little more than a handshake, too fast for anyone watching to see.

'And so the children behind the Iron Curtain – which is what the muffling of the culture of the rest of the world in Soviet places was called – began to hear songs. Just small, silly songs, songs that said 'I wanna hold your hand' and 'twist and shout'.

'But if you think that being small and silly meant that these songs weren't important, then you don't have the first idea of how music works. The government obviously did, otherwise why ban them in the first place?

'They were important because they taught kids to dance and sing and laugh and move and love; that there was more to life than being serious and obedient. Music taught them that they weren't alone. It made them see how the world might be.

'That's why the grey market's gonna live forever, no matter what anyone does to kill it. It's immortal.

'Art always finds a way. Art is how to fight a war without weapons. When we create, when we love, that's when we're not under their power anymore.

'And if you know anything about history then you already know that when the Iron Curtain fell it did so without a single bomb ever being launched.'

40

Ariette, Jesse and Eric teach Olivia the basics of Capoeira, a theatrical and acrobatic type of martial arts. They offer it to Sam as well, but he declines. Hannah teaches him how to shoot, instead.

Capoeira is a sneaky kind of dance, a tricksy game. It's impossible to do without understanding how people think, and the lies they want to believe about the world.

'It exploits expectations in the opponent,' Olivia notes after one lesson, stretching her exhausted muscles. Ariette nods, a pleased smile on her sharp face.

'Yes, exactly. You need the same kind of brain for it that you need for computer hacking,' she tells Olivia. 'That's how I knew you'd be a natural.'

The Capoeira lessons make Olivia athletic. She's never been athletic before. Muscles and grace replace the skinny coltish shape her body's always had until now.

She hates seeing Sam and Hannah with their guns. No matter how devil-may-care Hannah might work at seeming, Olivia remembers that kid who looked at a plate of food like it hurt her to see it. And no matter how much Sam might get cranky at her for it and tell her to cut it out, she looks at him and sees somebody she wants to protect and keep safe. To see the two of them with deadly weapons in their hands, working at improving their skills at using them effectively, hurts her deep in her heart.

Olivia would kill a thousand enemies if it meant that Sam and Hannah never had to fight a single one. She doesn't care at all how much blood she'd have to get on her hands, so long as they were shielded and safe.

'They're not your *pets*, Christ,' Ariette snaps one day, seeing the expression on Olivia's face as she observes Sam and Hannah firing at their targets across a parking lot. 'What kind of look is that?'

Olivia sighs, shooting Ariette a glare. 'Keep your voice down.'

'They're wearing ear muffs, they can't hear us.'

Olivia knows Sam would be affronted to see Olivia being weird and sentimental about him yet again. She thinks Hannah might get it, though. A little. She thinks Hannah might feel that way about Olivia and Sam, too, the burning need to keep them protected. It's just that in Hannah's view, that means arming them against the dangers they might face.

'Have you ever raised tomatoes?' Ariette asks her now, as they stand and watch. Olivia shakes her head.

'If you're too careful with them, if you treat them too well, they don't turn. Without adversity, they don't grow.'

'They're my friends, not fucking *tomatoes*,' Olivia replies.

Ariette shrugs. 'What? I was telling you about tomatoes, that's all. If you thought I was talking about something else, that's your problem.'

41

The market's a day trip away from the complex, a chance to barter with the other salvagers who eke out a living in these old suburbs. Olivia doesn't go often. She's not a skilled and seasoned pro at traversing the world like Hannah is, but she goes sometimes.

So much is there: relics and illegal objects and contraband items and old, worn, handmade curiosities, all laid out on tables or hanging on racks or pinned to the walls of canvas stalls and dilapidated caravans.

Books are greatly loved and highly prized, surviving the years better than more perishable media, better than music and film and television recordings. Out here, where readers don't work, there's an air of reverence around the battered, water-warped paperbacks which crowd boxes in the corners of stalls.

She has some savings from their time at the factory. Spending that hard-won, misery-earned cash on books for herself and for the complex makes some of the jagged ache in her heart fade.

When she buys a creased, yellowed copy of James Hilton's *Lost Horizon* one Saturday morning, the vendor tells her, 'This was the first pocketbook, you know. Well, not this one, this is obviously a much later edition. But this book. First mass-market paperback in the world.'

Olivia tries to imagine that. The promise, the hope that such a treasure must have embodied for those who had never before been able to afford books of their own. The freedom that a rectangle of cheap paper and cardboard and ink could provide.

She stays up almost until the light of morning reading the

novel. Gobbling books down in such large servings is a bad habit that she has no interest in curing herself of. She wouldn't feel like herself if she didn't do it that way, no matter how impractical and silly that way might be.

It seems perfect to her that this book was the first paperback; this story about exhaustion, the sense of growing old very fast, that comes with living after the time of the Wars. Olivia can relate to that very, very much. She wonders that a writer living right in the middle centuries of the Wars should understand so clearly what it would be like afterwards.

There is such a beautiful, poignant truth in the book's visions of a place where stories and learning survive, even when the rest of the world wanted all of it lost and forgotten and destroyed. This story calls the place *Shangri-La* but in Olivia's opinion it might as well be called *the complex*.

The place where happy endings live.

Olivia puts the paperback aside, curls up against Sam, and is so happy and so tired that she cries until she falls asleep, and dreams of nothing until the afternoon.

42

When the weather's chilly, there are bonfire nights on the sprawling rooftop parking lot of a gigantic, half-crumbled shopping mall. People drive and walk and ride from lots of far-away places to hang out together. It's a chance to see some unfamiliar faces for a change, after living in small to medium groups most of the time.

The fire pits are giant jagged craters where debris has hit the cement surface of the roof and gouged holes into it. A web of thin cracks go in all directions around each pit, and Olivia has a faint thrill of fear at the idea of the whole thing crumbling out from underneath them all. It never does, though. Any structure that's managed to survive this long is probably sturdy enough to last another few hundred years.

The triplets never come to bonfire night, for obvious reasons. Hannah and Sam and Olivia do sometimes, to sell food they've made, spreads and pies and popcorn and dried fruits. One of their customers gives them an old movie projector as payment. After that they collect canisters of film at the market whenever one shows up in working order.

Even with their diligent collecting, they never have a large collection by the standards of even the smallest legal archives back in the city. They manage to gather fifteen films – twelve of them intact from start to finish – and that's a bounty almost beyond imagining for the residents of the complex.

There's *The Crow*, all about love and revenge, a man who comes back from dying to paint his face in blacks and whites and burn down everyone who has earned his vengeance. And there's *Hook*, though the first and last reels are missing and so they have to make up their own end and beginning for it. It's a Peter Pan story, about the children who have to live in the ruins of the world left when the proper story's ended.

The Little Mermaid is intact but grainy and scratched, the cartoon colours faded and warped to acidic blues and greens for some parts, the music stretched out and wavering into wobbled, uneven notes.

The generally agreed-upon favourite of the collection is *Blade Runner*, which Hannah and Sam in particular watch whenever it's screened, on a strung-up canvas sheet in the courtyard after dark.

Olivia can never decide if she should step in and suggest they hold off watching it so often. Sam's getting obsessed with parts of it, especially this one scene where the hero is talking to the heroine, trying to prove to her that her memories aren't her own, that everything about her is borrowed from someone else's life, that she's not human at all.

He recounts her own memory to her, of watching a spider build a web outside her bedroom window.

The spider lays an egg, and then one day it hatches.

Every time they watch the movie, Sam recites the next lines along with the actors.

'The egg hatched,' he says under his breath, so only Hannah and Olivia can hear. 'And a hundred baby spiders came out. And they ate her.'

43

Olivia likes the quiet, likes being alone with herself. She likes exploring the empty, forgotten places that stretch in every direction around her home.

Sometimes, when she takes some of the jam she makes to the markets, she trades them for scavenged, dented old spray cans. She learns how to thin down ordinary house paint until it will work in old plastic plant misters, squirting out a fine rain of colour.

Olivia starts to decorate the ruins.

She knows better than to paint too close to home – the last thing they want is to draw attention to the neighbourhood around the complex. So Olivia treks out alone, further and further away each time that she can work up the requisite courage.

Just as the city once seemed infinite, back when she'd barely been outside its edges, Olivia finds herself marvelling at the apparent endlessness of the long-ago evacuated suburban sprawl.

It's nothing like those small pockets of ruins that were becoming less and less frequent through her childhood, the ones that could be walked through in the span of an evening stroll. These empty buildings often seem to go to the edge of the world, and then beyond that.

Sometimes Olivia makes murals, pictures from her dreams and the books she's read. Other times she creates patterns, or solid blocks, or gradients from one shade to another.

Olivia isn't sure what she'd tell anyone who asked her why she does it. Luckily, nobody asks. Maybe everyone understands, even if nobody knows how to talk about it.

44

Two suburbs over, and on the other side of one of the largest rubble piles visible this side of the horizon, is a museum. The roads and gardens that they have to drive through to get there have gone so wild that at times it's like trying to get through a forest or a jungle.

Olivia, Sam and Hannah push on through to find more scraps and shards of the ruined past that they can give away or keep.

A chess set made of red and white marble is there, the pieces carved with deep, rough lines. There's no board in the broken glass case, just the rows of pawns and nobles.

'Stupid,' Hannah remarks, putting the set into the satchel at her hip. 'I don't care how old or rare they thought it was. What's the point of a game that nobody's allowed to play?'

'The King is stationary in chess because people thought the most important bee in beehives, the one that never moved, was a King, you know,' Olivia says. 'It wasn't until way later that people realised that she was a Queen.'

'I haven't ever really played,' Sam admits.

'I can teach you,' Olivia tells him. 'I was a champion when I was a little kid.'

'I never knew that.'

'Yeah, I was pretty obsessed. I gave it up because, I dunno, I didn't like how it made me think. It's not the kind of logic I like. You need to be aggressive to be really good. Ruthless.'

Hannah smirks. 'Ariette would kick your ass if she heard you saying you didn't want to be like that.'

'Whatever, she always wants to kick my ass anyway.' Olivia shakes her head. 'Let's keep going.'

In the next room are wooden carvings, ornate and bewitching, decorated with impossible creatures. Sam stops in front of one, a grotesque chimera of fish and monkey and pig and crocodile parts, jaws stretching wide at either base with a freestanding doorway.

'*Torana,*' he reads from the plaque beside it, the beam of his flashlight illuminating the thick stirred-up dust in the air. 'It says this example here's a *makara*. It protects the entries to places. Cool.'

Olivia and Hannah exchange a glance. They're never absolutely sure in these moments if Sam totally understands that something is intended as a metaphor, a symbolic idea rather than literal truth.

But the big sign on the wall of the room says that the artefacts are all from Hindu and Buddhist temples. Those are religions, and Olivia knows that the whole metaphor/truth thing gets muddy when religion gets thrown into the mix.

Sam keeps reading. 'In Sri Lanka, colourful toranas lit up with glittering electric lights were set up in public places to mark the festival of Buddha's birth, enlightenment and death. People celebrated by creating public art and sharing food, doing their best to bring happiness to the people around them.'

'Wanna bring it home?' Hannah asks. Olivia and Sam both nod. The arch is incredibly beautiful and deserves to be somewhere alive and full of light, not here in the dark with heavy dust and silence.

They won't be able to fit much else on the utility vehicle they drove here if they take it, but that's okay. Most of the museum's smaller treasures are gone, picked up by scavengers who were here long before the three of them.

'Public art and sharing food,' Sam muses as they begin the mazelike drive back through the overgrown suburbs. He's sitting in the passenger seat beside Olivia, sketching in his pad as she drives. Hannah's riding on the flatbed back with their loot. She likes the wind in her hair, and to be able to see around them at all times. That's why they've taken to using the truck rather than the car, though Olivia's not as confident behind the steering wheel as Hannah.

It always feels like she's doing something super-illegal when she drives, as if her whole life now isn't varying shades of against-the-law.

'Those are what we do,' continues Sam. 'Graffiti and peanut butter.'

Maybe it's not so bad, if Sam really does believe that there'll be a monster protecting their home with the carving in place. If Sam or Hannah ever need a monster's protection, then Olivia will find a way to become a monster.

When they stop to refuel the truck from the plastic tanks, Sam shows them pages and pages he's drawn of how the arch will fit into the existing doorway of the apartment. Olivia wonders again whether Sam could have been an architect, if the world were different. It makes her heart feel like a knot pulled too tight.

So they get their new doorway, and find themselves falling into the habit of touching their fingers to the *makara*'s long jaw in greeting as they go in or out. It makes the apartment theirs in a way it wasn't before.

45

Olivia's mixing her thinned-out paint bottles in the courtyard one evening when Ariette comes to stand in front of her.

They've all kept on dyeing their hair in the same shades they chose on that first occasion, though the bullying that prompted it is long past. Olivia's so used to Ariette's blue-ocean hair that it's strange to remember it was ever otherwise.

'Would it be okay if I came too?' Ariette asks. As usual, her words are more a challenge than anything else, so it takes a second before Olivia realises that Ariette's asked her a question.

'Oh! Sure. Of course,' Olivia says, smiling. Ariette nods, not returning the smile, and walks away.

Still, the next time Olivia heads off on one of her treks, Ariette is there beside her.

They spend the first hours hiking along the cracked old roads without chatting much. Ariette's not in the habit of talking for talking's sake, and Olivia's used to the quiet. It's nice.

This time of year, lots of birds are out. At one point they see the squat brown shape of a wombat shuffling along on its own errands.

It always makes Olivia happy when she sees wildlife. Eric and Jesse, in their more unguarded moments, have told her a bit about what it was like following the burnout. About the burrow of baby echidnas that Ariette had loved to visit, high on the hill at the edge of their father's fields. About the sad, small bones, black against the grassless expanse of the scorched dirt in the same place. The smell of the koalas trapped in their trees, and how the three children had been put off eating meat for months thereafter.

Olivia wonders if Ariette's thinking about those things too, or if she's made herself forget it as a way to survive.

They hit one of the suburbs Olivia uses for her art as the sun sinks and the light is turning golden. There's more than enough to see by, though, even for Olivia's eyes, which are pretty useless as far as eyes go. She chooses a wall, drops her knapsack to the ground, takes out her colours, and paints.

The work Ariette begins is smaller-scale, across one of the weathered wood boards nailed up in an empty window-frame. She takes several tries to find one that isn't soft with rot. The one she winds up with only has moss and damp around the edges, even after all the wet winters that the street's been left untended.

Most of the rest of the building is gone. Olivia guesses there was a row of cheaply built shops that crumbled over time. Only the original facade at the front, built long before the rest, remains. It makes the street look like a movie set.

In red and gold swoops and scrolls, Ariette writes:

I hope that the leaving is joyful, and I hope never to return.

They work in silence until there's no light left save for the stars. Then they stop, eat the dinners they've brought along, and set up their sleeping bags across the seats of a long-abandoned car.

Olivia loves sleeping in empty places. Being alone has a different quality when it's somewhere like this. It's less lonely.

'Frida Kahlo,' Ariette says when they're lying down and settled for sleep. Olivia drifts in and out for a long time before dozing off properly on nights like this. She makes a small 'hm' noise to let Ariette know she's awake, then waits for the other girl to continue.

'What I wrote. Frida Kahlo wrote it in her diary before she died. Nobody's sure if it was a suicide.'

'I thought it was pretty,' Olivia answers.

After that they're quiet until they fall asleep. In the stillest, darkest hours of the night, Ariette wakes up screaming from a nightmare, but pretends to be asleep when Olivia asks if she's all right.

In the morning, Olivia decides to replicate some of *The Little Mermaid* as a mural. It's one of the on-land parts of the story, where the mermaid has traded her voice for feet, but the wavery blue-green of the movie print Olivia has watched makes the scene look as if it's underwater anyway, as she conjures it up from an old brick wall.

Ariette's expression is neutral, but Olivia knows her more than well enough by now to tell when Ariette's displeased: when it comes to Olivia, the correct answer is "pretty much always".

'What?' Olivia asks, trying and failing to hide her exasperation. 'What've I done to make you make that face?'

Ariette sighs through her nose. 'Nothing. Don't worry about it.'

'Oh, no, you don't get to make that Olivia's-an-idiot face yet again and not follow through. What did I do?'

'No, no, I swear it's not you. For a change,' Ariette smirks. 'It's just that Disney messed with the story so much, and it reminded me of this one episode of this shitty old cop show I used to watch all the time. It was called *Special Victims Unit* because all the crimes were super racy or perverted. This one episode I saw, the detectives had to go to a boarding house run by a woman named Mrs Haze, because her tenant had been killed.'

'Lemme guess, she had a teenage daughter named Lolita,' Olivia says, returning Ariette's smirk.

Ariette shakes her head. 'No, the teenage daughter's name was Virginia. Really clever covering of their tracks there, huh?'

'And the daughter's the killer?' asks Olivia.

Ariette nods. 'She strangles him.'

Olivia's read *Lolita*, by Vladimir Nabokov, where Charlotte Haze and the tenant and the boarding house have been borrowed from. She knows that the book is a big literary classic and everything, but to her it was at its heart the story of a girl that nobody loved enough, and who got hurt horribly by selfish people.

Olivia loves the idea of a show that gives Lolita the chance to strangle her mother's manipulative, heartless tenant to death.

'Cool. I hope to see it someday,' she says to Ariette. Ariette makes a noise of disgust.

'I should have known you'd think it was *cool*,' Ariette says, unable to stop herself from sneering. 'You never care about preserving the integrity of the fucking story. You're probably pleased that Disney gave *The Little Mermaid* a happy ending.'

'What the fuck's wrong with a happy ending?'

'You are the most indiscriminate consumer I've ever met!' snaps Ariette. 'What about showing some respect for the classic western canon?'

'*Respect* and *worship* are different things,' Olivia fires back. 'Why can't all the different shit that comes later get added into the mix too? Why can't it grow and change in ways that the listener wants?'

'Because classic, important stories aren't alive, jackass. Nothing immortal is alive.'

Olivia shakes her head. 'That's... pitiful,' she says. 'It's chess pieces in a glass case, without a board. Seriously, I genuinely pity you for thinking like that.'

Ariette makes an outraged bark of laughter at that but Olivia ignores it, speaking on without pause. 'You think stories just have one version, the one that got said first. You want *Peter Pan* but not *Hook*. Why can't Lolita get to be a murderer sometimes, instead of a victim? Why *shouldn't* we be allowed to tell our own new versions?'

'The canon-' Ariette begins again. Olivia shakes her head and returns to her painting.

'Fuck the canon,' she tells Ariette. 'I make my own truth.'

It's the last proper conversation they ever have.

46

Olivia has read so many stories that she's learned their common rhythms. Not only the "once upon a time" and "all lived happily ever after" parts, but the bits which live below the surface and dictate the shapes of actions.

She's spent so long learning those rhythms and rules that she expects some kind of foreshadowing before big events in her own life. Twists and swerves have to be telegraphed before they happen, or else they don't make *sense*.

But when Olivia looks back later, there's nothing. Real life doesn't have leitmotifs, and it doesn't give out warnings.

Esperanza and Ariette are heading to the connectivity margin line, to pick up a load of the manufactured perishables that the complex grudgingly gets from the city.

If they absolutely had to, they could live without sunscreen and toilet paper and toothpaste, but it seems petty to make their own lives a lot less comfortable just to avoid a small – and necessary – evil.

'I'm going to go too,' Sam decides, an hour before they leave. 'I want new pencils and pens, and I should check in with my old networks. I don't do that as often as I should.'

Olivia frowns. She hates that Sam maintains those connections to their old life. Does he think he'll need to go back someday, to resume those old patterns?

'I'll come along as well, then,' she says. Sam draws a deep sigh in through his nose.

'You're not my nanny.'

Olivia opens her mouth to launch into her standard protest at the accusation, then gives a sigh of her own and closes it again.

'Okay, fine. I'll see you when you get back.'

She goes to tend to the chickens, distracting herself from her habitual worry whenever she isn't at Sam's side.

Hannah had brought the chickens back from the market, when they'd been extremely small fluffy dinosaurs.

That's what Olivia had exclaimed the first time she'd seen them: 'Oh my god, they're tiny fluffy dinosaurs, oh my god.'

They were, in theory, the property of the whole complex, living in a wire-and-wood coop in the corner of the courtyard, but everyone had taken one look at Olivia's enraptured expression and understood who was in charge of them.

Their eggs are much smaller than the ones Olivia remembers from her long-ago breakfasts before school. The shells are different from those ones too, not only in size but in hue – speckled brown or a dark coffee-cream rather than the uniform off-white – and in thickness; much stronger than the eggs Olivia remembers, so much tougher to crack.

She collects the eggs in the early mornings, when the colours of the day are still muted and soft, the last stray stars visible in the sky. The little ovals fit easily into the cup of her palm, warm and new.

Depending on how many eggs the chickens have to offer, and what recipes Sam has planned, sometimes they have a few for breakfast. Olivia isn't sure how much of the delicious, wonderful taste of those breakfasts is because she's so happy and alive now, compared to that old existence, but even factoring that in, she thinks that these eggs are far tastier than what she used to think eggs were meant to be.

The chickens provide an excellent distraction from fretting about Sam. Hannah comes down and helps her, and then the two of them sit among the vegetables and soak up the thin sunshine.

'I've been thinking about getting tattoos,' Hannah says.

Growing up, Olivia never saw anyone with tattoos. The permanent mods that people in the city get are almost always beauty surgeries or portings. Here among the outliers, though, tattoos are common. Ariette has one behind her ear, in the soft hollow beside the hinge of her jaw: a little spider.

'Yeah? What do you think you'll get?'

Hannah shrugs. 'I don't know. I've got a plan in mind, but I need to talk to you and Sam about it first. I was thinking tha-'

A loud, indistinct shout comes from the direction of the front gate. The sound is unexpected and urgent enough to make Hannah and Olivia both freeze for a moment before they hurry towards it.

It's the three who went out, approaching down the road. Eric, taking his turn on lookout, was the one who'd cried out. Olivia immediately understands why. She gives a yelp of her own at the sight.

Sam is in the lead, with Esperanza trailing behind under the weight of carrying Ariette on her back. Sam's cradling his right arm against his chest. All three of them are covered in blood and dirt, their hair wild and clothes torn.

The frozen shock lasts only a second or so, and then Eric and Hannah and Olivia are all running towards them, yelling behind them as they do to summon the rest of the complex.

Hannah, fastest on her feet, reaches Sam first, so Olivia follows Eric as he runs on to Esperanza. He lifts Ariette in his own arms, and the way her head lolls back as he does makes Olivia's blood run cold.

'She passed out while we were in the car,' Esperanza says, doubling over and panting for breath now that her burden's off her back. 'It's a clean-up car, one of their little zippy ones. I stopped it a mile back and we walked here, but that's still too close, I gotta-'

'Are you hurt?' Olivia interrupts her. Esperanza shakes her head. 'Okay. You go back and get rid of their car. Drive it to… to that old museum. We'll come and get you soon.'

Esperanza nods and slow jogs back in the direction she's just come, looking like she's walked out of ground zero of a bomb blast.

Olivia turns towards the complex. Eric and Ariette are out of sight already, back inside where there are first aid supplies and other hands to help. Hannah and Sam are making their way at a slower pace, Hannah supporting Sam with an arm around his waist. Olivia runs to join them.

He looks at her, his eyes glazed, not quite focusing on her face. 'Hey.'

'Hi,' she says, trying to work out how to help him walk without hurting the arm he's keeping steady against his shirt. His hand is swollen in a loose fist, red and purple where it isn't obscured by bloodied scratches.

'I had to shoot with my left,' Sam says in a drowsy voice. 'I've never… I had to get up close, because I've never practiced. I didn't account for recoil, so it… I had to do a second shot. Ariette downed him but I had to end it, because he was… he was screaming, and I didn't account for the recoil…'

'Shh, don't think about it. Let's get you inside…' Hannah guides him forward and Olivia trails beside them, feeling completely useless.

'I need more help here!' Eric shouts from inside the ground floor apartment he shares with his sister and brother. 'Please!' His voice cracks on the word.

'Go,' Olivia says. 'You know more first aid than I do, but I know how to treat this.' She moves in beside Sam, taking on Hannah's position in supporting his weight.

Hannah hesitates, but then straightens her posture and nods, going to help Eric. Olivia helps Sam up the stairs to their own apartment, through their lucky arch that was supposed to protect them from bad things happening.

'They hit her with a pathogenic dart. In her shoulder,' Sam says as Olivia eases him into a chair at their kitchen table. 'It whistled when it went through the air.'

'Did you get hit by one?' Olivia asks, her hands freezing mid-air, her brain racing as she tries to remember the pathogen training she'd had at school. Fuck, *fuck*.

'No. The flatbed rolled on me. There's this, too.' He uses his shaky, unharmed left hand to lift the hem of his shirt. A jagged gash runs the length of his torso, bleeding sluggishly. 'It's not deep, just messy.'

'Kinda like me, huh?' Olivia quips, running water into a bowl and grabbing the first aid kit from the cupboard. Now that he's sitting still and she can get a better look, Olivia can tell his arm's broken, possibly in more than one place. She doesn't know how to judge the extent of the internal injuries to his hand.

Everything from the freezer becomes an ice pack. Olivia rests a bag of carrot sticks alongside Sam's purple-bruised forearm, a package of flour that they keep as a frozen emergency standby at his wrist, a handful of ice cubes wrapped in a cloth for his poor battered hand to rest atop.

'We could tell they were planning to follow us,' Sam tells her, as she cleans the skin gently. 'They watched us as we walked around the stores. So we doubled back and around on foot, then hid out for thirty minutes. They got in their car and drove away. We thought we were safe.'

The clean-up patrols are supposed to police the outer edges of the city, but they venture out past the pulse line to bully and blackmail outlier residents often enough to be notorious for it. Olivia's never heard of them going to such effort to hurt anyone before, though.

'I think they were just bored and annoyed,' Sam says, as though he can hear her train of thought. 'Everything was calm and orderly on the edge, so there was nothing for them to work off their energy. So they were looking for something with no consequences. I used to see it sometimes when I was alone. Thrives are as worthless as outliers in some places.' He laughs quietly to himself, a woozy uneven sound. 'Imagine if they'd known I was both.'

Olivia gently slips one of the rolled-up bandages from the first-aid kit under the curved fingers and thumb of Sam's wounded hand, supporting the shape it's curled into. Two of his fingernails are a dark purple colour and one has split in half vertically down the middle, blood oozing from the crack. Her hands shake as she wraps another bandage lightly around the damage.

He's gone quiet, watching her.

Sam's right hand is his drawing hand.

What if they've taken that away from him, too, when they've taken so much else already?

'Hannah and I were talking about tattoos, before. She wants one,' Olivia says. 'Do you think you'd ever get one?'

In a hospital there'd be x-rays and emergency surgery and painkillers and lots of people who knew exactly what they were doing. Here, there's just Olivia in a kitchen that smells of new bread, with a cheap box of bandages and antiseptic.

She takes a deep breath and keeps working.

'Maybe,' Sam says finally. 'We talked about it once, too. Her and me. We were listening to Beatles records and picking out what lyrics we'd get.'

'Yeah?' Olivia prompts. 'What'd you choose?'

She grabs two long wooden spoons out of the container of utensils by the stove, and positions them as splints for the fractures in his forearm. They have enough bandages for the task for the time being, but what about when they need changing in a few days? Some spare kits are in one of the stock houses down the road, but Olivia can't remember how many, or what condition they're in.

Stupid, stupid. They've all been so stupid, thinking they were prepared for whatever came their way.

'I was talking about you in the car today,' Sam says, not answering her question. 'With Ariette. She was saying... she said she was reading something and it made her think of you. She was reading *Hamlet*, and she said that she'd realised that she didn't want Ophelia to drown. She wished that… She said it made her think of you.'

'Yeah, she says that now, but I bet we still end up fighting about it the next time we talk,' says Olivia. She absolutely refuses to think about pathogenic darts, about what might be happening downstairs. Her focus is on Sam, on making sure his arm heals properly. 'Come on, spill on what lyrics you picked.'

Sam shakes his head. 'I think I'd like to just be quiet, now.'

She thinks he has a concussion, and aren't people with concussions supposed to stay awake? Or is it that they have to be allowed to sleep a lot, so that the brain can heal? Fuck, fuck, *fuck*, she can't remember which one it is.

Sam's head nods forward onto his chest. Olivia keeps on working until his arm and hand are dressed as best as she can manage.

She shakes him awake and makes him stumble, barely conscious, in to lie on the bed.

'You have to keep it higher than your heart,' she says, piling two pillows up at his side and resting his arm on top of them. 'I'll be back soon.'

They might need her downstairs. She needs to go out with the car and get Esperanza from the museum. She needs to clean the kitchen. So many things need to be done.

For a few minutes, Olivia stands there, looking at Sam, her skin sticky with his blood, and she wracks her memories for foreshadowing.

There isn't any, of course.

Hannah's sitting outside their front door, her back against the carvings. Olivia sits opposite her. They are a matched pair, a part of the design. Two bloodied girls with dull eyes and numb voices.

'I sent Jesse out,' Hannah says. 'I sent Jesse to get more first aid kits from the store house. We went through the supplies faster than I thought we would, and we needed more. So I sent him out and he wasn't there when she died. She died without him there.'

Olivia doesn't say anything for a long time. She doesn't know how long it is. Long enough that the sticky blood on her skin turns stiff and flaky.

'We need to go get Esperanza,' she says finally. 'Come on. I'll drive.'

47

Winter really, really sucks.

The cold makes Sam's slowly healing bones hurt around the clock, making him restless at night and withdrawn while he's awake. Sometimes Hannah and Olivia can't get a word out of him for days at a time.

It's too cold and wet to have outdoor movie nights during this part of the year, so Olivia points the projector at a blank wall inside their apartment and does what she can to compensate for the shorter focal length.

She thinks it's funny, how novels and films and everything from the days of the Wars always make out that hacking only happens with computers. As though it's the specific skills that matter and not the philosophy behind them.

Anything can be hacked, if it's governed by rules. Hacking just means getting around those rules without breaking the whole thing or getting caught. Recipes can be hacked. Conversations can be hacked – like in that *Lolita* scene that she and Sam fought about, in another world and another time. Machinery can be hacked. Projectors can be made to shine on nearby walls instead of distant screens.

Sometimes Sam puts on *Blade Runner* as soon as he gets up in the morning, and plays it through on an endless loop as the day wears on. Olivia hates him watching it over and over, but Hannah says it's fine. They have hushed, hissed arguments about it in the kitchen, while from the other room the movie's soundtrack clatters ever onward towards its dark conclusion.

A hundred baby spiders came out. And they ate her.

The line always makes Olivia think of Ariette now, who went by Arachne and had a spider tattoo behind her ear.

Olivia used to love stories where the hero had to give up everything in order to stay true to what they believed in. She doesn't anymore. Sometimes it really happens, sometimes people get killed for what they love, and it's not like in the movies; there's no tearful farewell and heroic music.

They just die, and the ones left behind have to live with it.

'The city's not going to be happy until we're wiped off the map completely,' Eric says one evening, as he watches Olivia try to herd her chickens into their coop for the night. He's drunk again. He's drunk a lot now. Jesse too.

All the wine bottles left to salvage from the ruins are vintage, these days. That's kind of funny, Olivia thinks. She doesn't mind it when Eric and Jesse get drunk. Her father used to drink after work sometimes, and those memories are the friendliest ones Olivia has of him.

'They won't be happy then, either,' Olivia points out. 'Because then who will they have to push around and hurt?'

'Thrives,' Eric offers with a hard, humourless smile. 'Factory workers. The poor. The sick. The—'

'Okay, okay, god.' Olivia shakes her head, laughing a little because they all learned long ago that sometimes you gotta laugh or you'll cry. 'You win.'

That makes Eric scoff a laugh of his own. 'I don't think any of us get to do that.'

Olivia goes back upstairs. The end credits of *Blade Runner* paint the wall of the darkened living room.

'It's funny how different movies can be about artificial intelligence,' Sam says, as if the two of them were mid-conversation and had paused for a minute, instead of this being the first time that Olivia's heard his voice in days. 'In some, like *Terminator* with SkyNet, or *Alien*, there's the idea that the AI would see little to no worth in humanity. Or else they're this

143

incredibly benevolent force, helping humanity evolve to a higher plane.

'But then there's *Blade Runner* – and they're just like us. They feel sad, they long for things, they make friends. They aren't good or evil, they're just us.'

48

Sam starts spending more time in the kitchen, less time watching his movies. He's teaching himself to do things with his left hand. They've all stopped kidding themselves that he's ever going to get full movement back in his right one. Hannah packed away all his drawing things, out of sight. Olivia had to go for a long walk that day, until she was far enough away that nobody could hear her when she sat on the ground and screamed and screamed and cried until her voice was gone.

Every day is and dark and dank and wet, and the dawns and dusks draw closer and closer together.

Olivia helps Sam in the kitchen, as much as he'll let her. They do what they can to make warm, filling meals out of the supplies they have, and they share the meals with everyone in the complex. It's not much, but it's something. It blunts the pointed melancholy that's settled over all of them.

One night, while everyone's huddled together in one of the living rooms, soaking in as much thin warmth from the old oil heater as they can before retreating to their beds, Jesse says, 'We need to have a party. Something to break the gloom.'

'Like a Saturnalia,' Eric agrees. They're the chattiest of the gathering, words coming easier to them than to the ones who're sober. 'They used to be held before the winter solstice – so right around now, when things are at their darkest. It's a festival of light. You turn everything upside down and inside out, to try to feel better instead of the worst. It'd be a nice fucking change.'

'All the rules get thrown away,' Jesse explains to them, hectic colour high on his cheeks. 'Masters used to have to wait on

145

their slaves and give them banquets. It was impossible to declare war during Saturnalia. Shit, if I had my way it'd be Saturnalia all the goddamn time.'

'Later on it was called the Feast of Fools,' Eric says. 'Young people got crowned as the Lords of Misrule in their town and wore masks and costumes, having dances and music in the halls of ancient churches.'

Hannah's eyes widen, her attention caught by the words. It makes Olivia grin, despite herself. Eric's said the magic word: *masks*. Hannah will go along with anything, if that's a part of it.

'Even later it was called Mardi Gras, but it'd started to lose its magic by then. It'd all been divided up, so some people were performers and others were just spectators. An *audience*.' Jesse spits the word like it tastes bad. 'We've got to do it the old way. Everyone involved. Nobody more important than anybody else.'

49

They all throw themselves into the plan, striving to pull themselves out of the worst of the winter. Olivia and Sam cook and bake and prepare so many dishes in the lead-up that they almost forget to be cold.

Hannah's out with a salvage party on the afternoon before the gathering, so the two of them are left to their own devices to get ready. Olivia lets Sam be in charge of making up their faces, so that the colours and textures will be ones that make him happy.

'It'll end up looking sloppy and stupid if I do it,' Sam says, his voice bitter. 'I can barely write my own name anymore.'

Olivia shrugs. 'So? Nobody's going to be marking us for precision, dumbass. Just try to enjoy doing it. It doesn't matter how it looks in the end.'

He works with his usual methodical care, of course. The only reason Olivia doesn't smile at that is because he'd get cranky at her if she kept moving her face while he was working.

When he's finished, and lets her look at them both in the mirror, the image makes her laugh out loud in delight. Olivia gives Sam a delighted hug, careful to keep their faces from smearing as she does.

'I knew you'd think they sucked, but laughing is pretty fucking harsh,' Sam deadpans, a quiet pride lurking under his flat tones.

'Shut up, you know that's not what I mean.'

There's no colour in the designs at all, just stark blacks and whites. The lines shake in some places, and the angles and curves are a little uneven, but Olivia thinks that these things make the whole even more beautiful. She has to blink to stop her eyes from stinging. If she cried and ruined the design, Sam would never forgive her.

Sam's face is Pierrot the clown, dark lips in a cupid's bow and thick liner around his eyes, tiny black teardrops on each paper-white cheekbone.

Olivia's face is a replica of the facepaint worn by the title character in *The Crow*, a long thin mouth and sunken, skull-like eyes slashed through with sharp black lines.

They look like children and like monsters, all at once.

The party is in full swing by the time they make their way to the winter-barren courtyard. Esperanza has her guitar, and she and Jesse are singing. Eric is clapping along, completely out of time, making the two performers laugh and breaking their concentration.

Esperanza sees Olivia and Sam as they join the throng, and blows a kiss in their direction. Olivia can sense herself blushing under her paint.

Martin and Lin and Veronica, and all the other people that Olivia doesn't know as closely as she knows her friends, are dancing by the light of what seems to Olivia's dazzled eyes to be a thousand candles.

Everyone is made up with fantastical designs, and everyone is beautiful.

Hannah arrives with the other scavengers later, her face painted into a vibrant orange and pink sugar skull, the petals of a stylised flower across her forehead like a crown. It's the first time Olivia's seen Hannah publicly identify with her Latina ancestry, and it gives Olivia a sudden sweet pang for her own family. She is thinking about them more and more, lately.

Hannah's torn silk dress, like her face paint, reminds Olivia of a flower; a ragged-petal one bruised by the rain. She and Sam and Olivia all gravitate to one another, smiling delightedly as they examine the details of each other's new faces.

There's a small, dark, jagged piece deep down inside Olivia, a part that's always lonely, that's lonely even now. This part of her is always at one remove from the rest, observing the world around her with a sharp clarity that she's usually not at all grateful to possess.

Now, that little part of her pricks at the edges of this bright and happy moment and tells her that, in all the life ahead of her, this moment will be one of her most treasured and bittersweet memories: three laughing friends in painted masks in the evening light.

50

She's always a kid again, when she dreams about the dead maskers. Olivia thinks that's her mind's way of making sure that she never gets any older than the bodies around her, the ones that never had the chance to get anywhere past this moment: fox, mouse, cat.

Sometimes the mouse is Sam, which is the worst of the variations that the years have offered her. This time she's spared that particular nightmare, but the fox has indigo-blue hair and paint splatters on its hands along with the blood, which is just as bad.

The dream itself isn't anything new, but when Olivia wakes up from it, the idea is there in her head, as smooth and formed as an egg.

All day, she tries to find the right moment to talk to Hannah and Sam about it, but things keep getting in the way. She is more and more anxious about it the longer she puts it off.

So while Sam's cooking dinner, Olivia goes to the library, collects Hannah and makes her come upstairs to sit in the kitchen too.

'I need to...' Olivia starts, biting on her lip as she fumbles for the best words. 'I want to see my parents. I've been thinking about them a lot. I'm going into the city.'

'You're not going to see your parents.'

Olivia's so thrown by Sam's derisive snort that she takes a second to respond. 'You can't–'

'You're going to exchange stilted emails with them,' Sam clarifies. 'Small talk and manners and ten per cent genuine emotion, if that. The messages will go back and forth between you consistently, but nobody will ever suggest the possibility of meeting up.'

One thing that books almost never discuss about love, Olivia thinks, is how much of it is embarrassed resentment that someone can know you so utterly, whether you want them to or not.

'What's your real reason?' Hannah asks, her voice icy and sharp. 'Are you going to come back?'

Olivia looks down at her hands. Her cheeks are hot; she knows she's blushing.

'I don't know. I want… Eric said something and it made me think. We need to be off the map. This whole area, as far as possible in every direction. The city needs to think we're a toxic waste hazard, that we're radioactive, that… shit, I don't know. They need to think that it's a no-go zone.' She curls her fingers into fists, then uncurls them slowly, and can't look up. She can't meet their eyes while she says all this. 'I don't know what making that happen is going to involve, but I think Carabosse can–'

'Stay away from Carabosse,' interrupts Hannah. 'Fucking *look* at me, Olivia.'

Olivia looks up. Hannah points at the scar that bites deep across the flesh of her cheek. 'The price is always higher than you expect. You're too stubborn to give up on this idea now that you've had it, I know that much, but if you give the tiniest shit about making it back here, ever, you will do it without Carabosse.'

'I should tell them that Ariette–'

'Carabosse *does not care*. Ariette was just another good little pawn to push around their chessboard. The city eats kids like us alive and Carabosse gets to keep on playing, because idiot chumps like you show up to replenish the ranks.'

A hundred baby spiders. 'That's not what happened. Ariette didn't die anywhere near the city.'

Hannah gives a scoffing laugh, a sob lurking underneath, and looks away from Olivia. 'How long do you think it'd possibly last? Three or four years, maybe? Is that worth dying for?'

'It'd give you time to get strong enough to defend yourself in the longer-term. People could band together, and... Hannah, we need to grow, to *build*. Not just keep up with surviving. This would be a way to start a chance for that.'

'You can't go,' Sam says quietly. Now none of them are looking at each other. It would hurt too much to speak, if they did. 'I won't let you. I need you here.'

'You can't spend our entire lives insisting that I'm not your nanny, and then change your mind when it suits your argument.'

'You're not the complex's nanny, either! You're not the entire fucking world's nanny! This isn't your job!' he snaps, furious. His good hand flutters anxiously.

'Someone has to,' Olivia says quietly. 'Someone has to be the guardian in the doorway.'

'But why does it have to be *you*?' Hannah asks. Her eyes blink down, spilling the first tears of the argument. That sets Olivia off as well, almost instantly.

Sam doesn't cry, but Olivia knows him well enough to know that his heart's breaking, too.

Nobody says anything else. There's too much, and nothing, to say.

51

Esperanza drives her to the city outskirts. They go in the same car that Olivia and Sam made their first journey in, when Hannah came to the factory to find them. Everyone stopped using the car much after they got the flatbed, but now the flatbed's gone along with so much else, so the car's back to being their main long-distance transport.

It's a quiet journey. All Olivia's words have dried up. She feels hollow inside. She's surprised her heartbeat doesn't echo when it beats, that there's anything inside her to cushion and muffle the sound.

When they stop, finally, on the outskirts, Olivia struggles to find something to say to Esperanza. 'Thank you for the lift.'

There are tears on Esperanza's face. It strikes Olivia as miraculous, in a horrible way, how endlessly deep sorrow is as a wellspring. Characters in books sometimes run out of tears, but it never seems to happen in the real world. There are always more to be found, when the next thing happens.

They both lean in at once, almost close enough for Olivia's cheeks to dampen with borrowed tears, and as their mouths meet Olivia thinks *my first kiss, and it's a goodbye one.*

52

Nightfall comes early, so she doesn't make it very far inside the city limits before she has to stop to sleep. There are places to buy beds for the night, but they look and smell too much of the factory dormitory and she can't go back to a place like that. Not for this first night, anyway. Not when she began the day between Hannah and Sam with each of them clinging to her in their sleep, their stale morning breath puffing against her and making her make a face in annoyance.

If she has to go straight from that back into a dormitory-world, she might not find it in her to struggle upright again come morning. And she has to keep going, no matter what. There's no turning back now.

Instead of paying for a bed, she walks the dusky streets until she finds a half-collapsed house that nobody's bothered to rebuild. It's overgrown, gone to seed and mildew, so she knows there won't be squatters inside already.

Olivia doesn't bother to check the bedrooms, but heads instead for the bathroom, curling up in the tub with her backpack under her head and her jacket pulled over her for warmth. The cold of the porcelain beneath her makes her shiver, but she's glad of the distraction.

In the morning, she walks until she finds a café and buys a bowl of porridge and some connectivity time. Everything's wired, this far out in the suburbs – only inner neighbourhoods and the city proper are far enough from the pulses to use widespread wireless.

It used to seem so antiquated to her – the idea of accessing the online world from specific locations, of having a fixed point as its gateway, rather than being everywhere all the time.

But after spending so long without any digital technology at all, Olivia's given up on taking one state of affairs for granted and judging anything else in comparison to it. She's going to start over from zero, and look at every situation as an opportunity to hack things into what she wants and needs.

It isn't hard to find her old haunts on the grey web. She doesn't recognise any names in the chats, but that's no surprise. Technology moves even faster than the physical world, and even by those standards Olivia's been away a long time. She decides on Donkeyskin for her new name, and gets to work.

Ellie doesn't work in the factory computer division anymore, under Olivia's name or her own, but enough of an information trail is left in her wake that Olivia can track her from that job to the next one, and then the next.

This is a different kind of Capoeira to the one Olivia has learned to accomplish with her body, but the rules remain the same. Manipulation and subterfuge. If she can't play a simple computer system, she's never going to have a chance against a person, or lots of people.

Ellie is working at an investment bank now, as a personal assistant to one of the executives. Olivia writes down the information with pen and paper – it's going to take her a while to get out of the habit of making hard copies – and notes with a distant, detached part of herself that the offices are in the same part of the city as her father's corporate headquarters.

All of her is distant right now. If she thinks about anything in too much context, she's going to stop moving, and she has to keep moving.

She finds a board that's done the pig test in the last half-hour and come up clean. Then, in a private message to herself, she writes *Once upon a time, Arachne found an enchanted spindle.*

Less than five minutes goes by before a blank box pops up on her screen and text appears inside it.

Olivia?

Donkeyskin: Why do you assume that, rather than Ariette?

Does it matter?

Donkeyskin: Humour me.

You have a flair for the dramatic that's all your own. Is that good enough?

Donkeyskin: Fine.

Donkeyskin: It's me.

Donkeyskin: Olivia.

Donkeyskin: Did Bowdler save Ophelia?

Donkeyskin: He's the one who messed with the plays to make them family-friendly, right? That's where the word 'Bowdlerise' comes from, to mean censoring in the name of making stuff all fluffy and dumb?

That's correct.

And while Bowdler did alter her death, removing any implication of suicide.

No. He didn't save her.

Why do you ask?

Donkeyskin: It doesn't matter. I was just wondering.

She told Hannah that she wanted to inform Carabosse of Ariette's death, but now that she's got her fingers on the keyboard and the opportunity to do it, Olivia doesn't want to. She feels it is the final thing that will make it really, absolutely true.

It's exactly the kind of silly, dramatic thinking that Ariette was so scornful of, but Olivia can't help it. She doesn't have it in her to submit to this final letting-go, not right now.

Instead, she takes a deep breath, and reminds herself that she has to keep moving. Momentum is the only thing that'll save her now.

Donkeyskin: I need your help with something.

53

Olivia's imagined Carabosse a bunch of different ways at different times. Sometimes she imagines someone slim and chic, androgynously gorgeous and aloof at a bank of cutting-edge technology. Sometimes she imagines a kid not so different from her, some girl at a keyboard with too many thoughts to ever be content. Or a man like her father, powerful and ordinary at the top of an empire.

Usually though, Carabosse is the same blurred almost-concept of a person that anyone Olivia interacts with online becomes in her head. She knows that they have a name and a face and a body and a life, away from the computer, but those things are irrelevant to the version of them that she knows.

Carabosse is the name of the fairy in *Sleeping Beauty*, the one who wasn't invited to the new baby's christening along with the rest of the fairies in the kingdom. The invited fairies all give the baby gifts like beauty and golden hair and a sweet laugh, and then Carabosse shows up and her present to the little princess is "you'll prick your finger on the spindle of a spinning wheel on your sixteenth birthday, and die".

The other fairies manage to downgrade it to "sleep until you get woken up by true love's kiss" instead of "die". So of course Sleeping Beauty gets to sixteen, pricks her finger, and sleeps for a hundred years before she's woken up.

The cartoon version changed the fairy's name from Carabosse to Maleficent. Olivia thinks – with a tug in her heart that she now understands will be there for the rest of her life at times like this – that Ariette was probably pleased that the online user

Carabosse went with the classic name rather than the revision.

When Olivia first found out where the name Carabosse came from, while reading a book of fairy tales in the library at the complex one slow, sunny afternoon, it had seemed a weird name choice for someone to go by.

But after she thought about it, Olivia decided she liked it. The gift Carabosse gave Sleeping Beauty wasn't something that anybody in their right mind would want, but it was only because of it that Sleeping Beauty got a happy ending – without it, she would have lived and died before the prince was ever born, and never known what she didn't have.

It made Olivia think of being kidnapped, of how terrifying and uncomfortable and awful that experience had been. Nobody would ever *want* that. But if Olivia *hadn't* had to go through it, then she never would have met Hannah. She never would have cared about reading, and therefore met Sam. She'd have lived her whole life and never known that things were missing from it.

The new Carabosse, the one that's words on Olivia's screen and otherwise a mystery, says that her plan is possible. Difficult, but possible.

It's going to take a lot of work and a considerable amount of time to accomplish.

Donkeyskin: I figured. I don't care. I want it done. I'll help with whatever else you want, in the meantime. I'll make this worth your while.

Donkeyskin: I know you told me back then that you don't work on debts and owing like that, but I'll still do it.

All right.

54

So Olivia, who has been a child heiress and a kidnap victim and a high-school rebel and a factory girl and an outskirter scavenger and sometime baker, adds *civic infiltrator* to her list of identities.

When she lived in the complex, every part of Olivia's life was interwoven with herself: the gleam of pans and pots in the kitchen, the smell of books, the sounds of the chickens in the morning. The touch of the doorway under her fingertips whenever she went in and out of her home. The soft puff of Sam's breathing at night while he slept, and Hannah's hard, wild smiles, sharp and fast as lightning. The texture of the paint as Olivia covered all the grey that she could find with better, brighter hues.

Here, everything inside Olivia has been wrenched away from her, locked away in a chest. And she relinquished the key, she gave up all of that willingly. She chose to come here, to the blankness, to the nothing.

She contacts Ellie and gets a job doing data entry at the lowest level of the firm that Ellie works for. Her job is easy and repetitive and dull, no different to the computer work she'd been stuck with back at the factory before she'd found Hannah again.

Olivia's real work, done in evenings and in the quiet, lonely hours of the very early morning, is challenging, and she's glad of that. With hard work to do, she has less time and energy to feel lonely and sad.

The workload fluctuates: some nights, every pathway she opens in the security system is shut down in minutes, leaving her to hunt and troubleshoot new routes and flee from inquisitive scanning systems trying to pinpoint her location.

And then there are times when there's nothing to fix or destroy or reroute, no information she can alter. The world merrily transmits data back and forth, and Carabosse has to tell her to be patient, that their chance will come, she just needs to wait. It leaves nothing for Olivia to do except wander the empty rooms of her fake life.

She gets new glasses. The optometrist says that her prescription should have been updated long ago. The optometrist doesn't sound scolding, only sad. It's not uncommon for people to go year after year with out-of-date glasses. It costs so much to get new ones.

Olivia had been worried, before her appointment, that not having recent glasses would give her secrets away, but now she can see how stupid that fear was. There is absolutely nothing remarkable about poverty.

When she reads at night by the strong lights in the little room she rents to live in, with her new glasses on, she never gets even the slightest headache. She hates that. She hates that there's anything good at all in the city, anything that's better or easier than out at the complex.

If only things were simple, black and white, with one way of living as "bad" and the other as "good". But the city has so many tiny, useful things – eyeglasses and tampons and antibiotics and hot running water. And there had been unkind people out in the outskirts, the same as in the city – bitchy assholes who teased Hannah about putting henna in her hair, or people who stared at Sam when he flapped his hands.

Nothing's simple, nothing's easy, and Olivia is very tired.

55

Olivia learns about dead drops, which are hollow bricks and rocks where information or messages can be left and picked up. She learns about dry cleaning, which is a way to check if anyone is following her – a route so roundabout and narrow that anyone on her tail will become obvious. She meets other hackers who work with Carabosse, though never Carabosse.

Olivia works hard to be good at all of it, because if she isn't, then giving up all the things she's given up will be for nothing. She has to make this work she does worth the high price it has already cost.

But she is so lonely, and so out-of-place. She looks at the throngs of people on the trams and sidewalks and cafes, in elevators and shops. Everyone is so immaculately presented and tidy and uniform, groomed and neat and turned out in clothes which have only the most minute variations from those worn by the people around them. Suits and skirts and heeled shoes and silky stockings. Taupes and greys and silver-blues. Neckties.

Olivia wonders if she would be less lonely if she was like everyone else. If she stopped wearing her anonymity as a necessary disguise, and truly became what she is pretending to be.

She writes to her parents and asks them for some money. They send it, and don't suggest that she should come visit them. She doesn't suggest it either.

She gets her hair cut sleek and smooth and it smells like chemicals; she gets her nails buffed to a shiny sheen that reminds her of the sugar glaze on a cupcake. Her teeth are given veneers which make them white and straight as little fences. Little porcelain bullets in a row behind her glossy smile.

Only Olivia doesn't smile.

She has never been so unhappy.

56

In stories, people survive when they are desperately unhappy by keeping busy. They lose themselves in the present, in the moment at hand. Olivia tries to be mindful in this same way.

In her lunch breaks, she sits on the benches along the main street near her office and watches the world. There aren't any trees except in the greenhouse corridors high above, but somehow she can tell from the air that spring is fighting its way out of winter. Olivia turns her face to the light like a flower seeking nourishment.

The air is cool, but no longer uncomfortably icy. The "walk" and "don't walk" signs at the corner crossings make for fits and starts in the ranks of business-suited people tramping past. In their dark clothing they are like silhouettes. High heels make a more precise sound on the pavement than the flat shoes worn by men. The empty place inside her yawns so huge and hungry that she is surprised it doesn't choke her.

Being invisible, being Donkeyskin, is lonelier than Olivia ever imagined. People cough on her in crowds, not registering her presence as something to avoid coughing on. Their gazes slick away from her like water off greaseproof paper.

Sometimes she feels so adrift, her body so anonymous, that the only way Olivia can become real again is to hurt herself. Every careful cut of the surgery-sharp scalpel blade against her skin regains a little territory, gives her back dominion and control. The pain reminds her that she exists.

The cuts heal, eventually, and leave behind thin scars of white and pink. Olivia wonders if she'll live long enough, be miserable long enough, for her to paint her whole body with criss-cross marks.

At night, rain lacquers the roads dark and glossy with the occasional flash of oil-slick rainbow, and every beam of light paints out a long straight halo of reflection below it – amber traffic lights, white headlights of cars, the multicolour glow of shop signs and the electric spill from interiors through glass doors.

Steam, exhaust and raindrops give the air a chilly, compassionless romanticism. The poetry of the city.

It's harder and harder to read most of the books she has, sanctioned and illegal alike. When she tries, they seem trite and irrelevant and pointless. Even stories which have always made her feel full up with riches are now so much sawdust to her soul.

The only novel she manages to read from start to finish is *American Psycho* by Bret Easton Ellis, which sickens her and gives her nightmares. Her dull revulsion at its deadened horrors is the only response to literature that has any authenticity to her.

Olivia finds a chill but honest comfort at the thought that some writer so long ago, back in the days of the Wars, could capture with such sharp perfection the shallow evils of life.

The year limps to a close, exhausted and sad. Olivia stands by the window of her little room and watches the fireworks through the glass. The explosions light up the miasma of pollution in the clouds, giving the colours a sickly tint.

57

In ancient fairy stories, January is the time of sea monsters. That's what Capricorns are, the star sign for the month, monsters that are made of two creatures together that swim in the dark. It makes her think of the wood carving with its watchful monsters, the *makara*. That's the word for January in the Khmer language.

Olivia thinks it's funny that people talk about Halloween as the time when the barrier between the real and the unreal is at its thinnest, when January is named for Janus, the god of transitions. Of doors and doorways, time and endings, gates. Janus has two faces so that he can look forward and backward all at once. The title *janitor* comes from Janus, for the one who care-takes and cleans.

January is her time. She is the care-taker. She is the monster in the doorway. She is a dark bubbling cauldron of terrible things, kept just out of sight by the hazy grey of surviving one day at a time, invisible in a city filled to spilling by the invisible. Crowds composed entirely of those who don't exist.

If she isn't human, she'd rather be monster than wraith. She's tired of hating herself. She resolves to hate them instead: for not seeing her; for ignoring the fact that every anonymous soul in a throng is as complex and precious and strange as themselves; for only deigning to recognise the existence of those who had by luck and circumstance managed to fit the punishing criteria of being worthy, being beautiful and whole.

If this is survival of the fittest, then to hell with evolution. Olivia will be a meteor among them, and revel at the wasteland in her wake.

58

She takes a risk and sells a few of her paperbacks. It isn't hard to find a dealer. The prices she gets are almost worth giving up the stories she treasured so much.

The food she buys with the money is simple, filling, healthy stuff. Ingredients that might have come from the complex's own courtyard garden, and probably came from somewhere just like it. They cost her most of the small illicit fortune she's earned. Carrots, potatoes, beans, onions. She manages, barely, to afford salt and pepper and stock as well. Brown rice.

A small and knotty pumpkin is for sale, but Olivia regretfully puts it back. Her money isn't infinite. Next time, she consoles herself.

What she cooks is somewhere between a soup and a stew and a risotto, but whatever it is, it's warm and thick and good. She buys a stack of paper bowls and a clutch of plastic spoons, then carries everything down to the dark corners, where most of the thrives make their homes.

The kids come quickly. She knew they would. Bad hunger has a kind of nihilism about it. Olivia has never forgotten that, and never will. There comes a point where you don't care what you're going to have to do as payment, or if the mouthfuls you're gulping are poison. It doesn't matter at all so long as the emptiness goes away.

The pot, huge as it is, depletes quickly. Word travels and the little crowd grows.

'Why?' one of the kids asks her, a thousand questions wrapped into one. Olivia shrugs.

'I missed feeding people,' she answers.

She sells more books the next day. She makes another pot, and gets more bowls and spoons. Maybe she can ask people to bring their own crockery and utensils, so she'll have more money for ingredients.

This whole scheme is out of step with the bland, carefully ordinary persona she lives behind now. The old Olivia would do it; the girl who cooked and laughed and loved and had a decorated face as she danced with her friends.

At the last moment, she buys two tubs of children's face-paint with the last of her money.

Kids and adults are already waiting for her when she delivers her new pot that night. Some of them have bowls and spoons. A few have brought bread, and give her the small, hard loaves to share out among the crowd. The generosity makes a lump choke up Olivia's throat but she blinks the tears away so as not to ruin her mask.

'You're like the clowns with food carts at old circuses,' one man tells her with a grin as she fills his bowl, 'With trays of sweets and corn and sausages. The candy butchers.'

'Candy butchers? Why'd they get called that?' Olivia asks him.

He shrugs, mouth already full. 'Don't know. They just were.'

'Well, sorry to disappoint, but the soup's vegetarian. I'm no butcher,' Olivia jokes, and moves on to serving the next person in line.

The name sticks in her head, though. When someone asks her a few nights later what her name is, she smiles behind her black and white paint and ladles food into another bowl and answers, 'Call me the Candy Butcher.'

59

This is extremely reckless.

Donkeyskin: In contrast to this stuff I do with you and the other hackers, which is incredibly safe and legal.

When was the last time you had any kind of vaccination booster? Was it when you were in the hospital for observation after your kidnapping?

Donkeyskin: Yeah probably. Maybe at school after. I don't remember.

Donkeyskin: If you're about to tell me that thrives are all dirty and diseased I will hunt you down and break your nose.

No.

But there isn't any herd immunity in the thrive population. On the contrary, a significant portion of the criteria for designating someone as a thrive centres around conditions which make people especially susceptible to illness and infection.

It's like the old saying about island communities: you catch a cold, then it's everyone's cold.

60

The lower tiers don't have many health clinics. The few that struggle on are stretched to breaking, not enough resources and too many desperate patients in need of help.

Olivia has precious little free time left, between the espionage work she does for Carabosse, her day job in the data entry centre and her nights spent wreathed in paint. But keeping busy is the only way she's holding on to any sanity, so she relinquishes the time gladly and helps out.

The first job the clinic gives her is photocopying pamphlets and doing net postings. An embarrassed nurse's aide asks her if she's ever heard of the pig test.

'It's not that we want you to break any laws,' he assures her hurriedly, as she bites back a smile, 'It's that... this shit is so important for us to get out there, and any education programs we try to run get shut down. They say it's because they don't want to cause a panic, but it means people don't *know*, and we need people to know.'

So Olivia does her digital Capoeira, flitting underneath the beam of the government's searchlight, and posts the messages online. She photocopies piles of one-page information sheets and then mixes pots of watery paste, gluing the clinic's health recommendations over advertising posters and concert fliers and boarded-up windows.

She paints her face in angular, exaggerated versions of Pierrot designs to do the real-world stuff, so that the facial recognition cameras can't identify her. Now that she's wearing different masks all the time, Olivia understands why Hannah loved being the red rabbit so much. The paint is so much more freeing than the subtle tones of the makeup she's expected to wear at work. The paint feels more like her face than this normal daytime disguise ever could.

The clinic sends endless pleas to central supply firms, asking for disposable needles they can distribute, and for antibiotics and antiretrovirals and vaccines and a dozen other vital things. If it's a good month, they get maybe a tenth of what they've asked for.

Olivia can't even pretend to be shocked by these things anymore. The days when she was naïve enough to have any faith in the world are long, long gone.

One night she's in a club, listening to the music of the band onstage and wishing that it made her feel something, *anything*. She wonders if that desperation for sensation counts as a feeling of its own, but decides a few seconds later that it doesn't. That'd be like saying that drowning was a kind of breathing.

On one of the walls, where she'd tacked some of the clinic's sheets a week before, someone has scrawled across the information in photoluminescent paint. It glows in eerie, sickly shades in the black-light of the dancefloor.

LOVE IS A VIRUS

She wonders what the writer meant by it. To her, it says that the things people try to find meaning and fulfilment and a reason for living in are all toxic, in the end. Love is a disease that you'll just pass on like it was passed to you.

The detached part of her, always off at one remove from the rest of her mind and heart, scoffs at her nihilism. She's come a long way down since that morning when she yelled at her father across the breakfast table for his nasty cynicism about the world. He probably didn't have half the contempt for the human race that Olivia has these days.

Olivia tries to think of her friends at the complex, the people she'd loved enough to come here for. They, at least, should be a bright enough light to sustain her through this dark.

But when Olivia thinks of Esperanza, she thinks of the

padding Esperanza put into her bras and at her butt to create the shape her heart knew her body was meant to have. When she thinks of Jesse, it's of the snug sports bras he'd worn double-layered so he'd feel a proper fit inside his clothes. What did kids like them do in the city? Did they run away, or try to contort themselves into what the world was insisting was correct for them? Did their families cut them off, leaving them to fend against the world like the more officially recognised categories of thrives? Or, faced with these as their possible fates, did the kids simply opt out entirely, ending their own lives?

It makes her weep to think about, those other Esperanzas and Jesses, other Sams, other Hannahs, who were born so deprived that there wasn't even anything to arbitrarily take away if they didn't measure up.

Life has no fairness to begin with, she writes in giant white letters across the dark wall beside a busy underpass, *and we make it infinitely worse.*

61

One day on her lunch break, Olivia is out walking, and from across the street she sees a familiar face. It's one of the assembly line supervisors from the factory. Not one of the worst, not one of the kindest. Just someone who doled out petty cruelties without thinking much about them one way or the other.

She doesn't approach him or follow him, though she wants to. She wants to hurt him. She wants to hurt him very, very badly.

There's always been a violence inside her, when she's at her angriest, but it's never felt like this before. The hard, heavy egg of misery in her ribcage has hatched, and the thing inside it is clawed and fanged.

She always knew that something in her was a harpy, a mermaid, a gryphon. A half-girl monster in the doorway.

She goes home. She chops vegetables. She works her way methodically and carefully through her checkpoints online, cauterising threats. She makes soup. She reroutes a patch to a quieter data zone. She paints her face.

When the soup's all served and eaten, later in the night, Olivia takes to the rooftops and starts teaching herself the old Capoeira moves, adjusted for her older body and its different centre of gravity, its new weight distribution.

The city has a second, secret beauty up here, one that's never visible from the ground. A world of balconies and stairs and fire escapes, of windows and apartments and a tangle of different skyline heights. The air is cleaner up here. Olivia takes deep breaths.

There. Down in a quiet and darkened street. A man, trapping a woman into a tight corner with the bulk of his body, holding her arms out of the way with one hand as he tears at her clothes with the other.

Olivia doesn't let herself feel anything. Luckily, the numbness comes easy. Good. She hopes she never feels anything again.

She drops from the rooftops to the street, bouncing from level to level down the fire escape as fast as she can manage. The soles of her shoes are nearly silent as she lands, but the man hears anyway and turns.

His hands are half-curled, fingernails hooked to gouge, swinging for her eyes as he steps in closer and tries to set the terms of the fight.

Eyes, throat, crotch, ankles. Olivia remembers the list from her self-defence class at school. She wonders if the lesson has ever saved any of the people preyed on by this man.

His nails scrape two lines through the paint and skin on her cheek, dragging white smears across his fingertips and Olivia grabs his wrist and squeezes, grinding the bones together. The shout growing in his mouth dies half-born.

Later, when Olivia's in the bathroom she shares with the other boarders in her building, the door locked against intruders, she'll touch her fingertips to two bright new scratches on her cheek, smearing her paint in the wound and making the cherry colour of the blood turn a watery pale red, clumpy with makeup.

The strength, the lividity of the shade, will make her sick and dizzy, the way Sam used to feel when he had to wear anything too colourful and bright.

No, not "used to". He almost certainly still does, so there's no reason to use past tense. But it's hard to think of Sam like that, or Hannah. Olivia's life now is another world entirely. Another time, as well as another place.

Later, she will paint over the cuts, obliterate their brightness with a thick coat of stark white.

She will hardly feel the fever-burn of infection that comes after. It doesn't matter.

But that's later. Now she's on a dark street, the pavement damp on her socks through her sneakers. A knife is in her hand and it's slicing the man's soft, sleek throat open, lurid technicolour red spilling everywhere, staining everything to wet black in the street lights.

The woman he was trying to hurt looks at Olivia with something like love.

'Thank you,' the woman says, quietly, and runs away.

Olivia looks at her hands, gloved in red, and she laughs and doesn't stop until she vomits.

Later, after she's put more white over the red lines on her face and scrubbed her hands until they feel clean again, she curls in the corner of her room, back to the wall and knees to her chest. She shivers until morning comes.

When the sun's out, Olivia knows she has no choice but to wipe away the comforting white and black of her mask and replace it with the light, sweet-smelling foundation designed to erase identity rather than create it. The smooth weightless glide across her features, forehead and cheeks makes her prickle and itch. Her glossed mouth trembles, and she bites her lip.

The cuts have scabbed over, inflamed and sore, but a swipe of sickly green concealer renders them invisible and neutral again. Under other circumstances Olivia might be glad to see the fever-pink gone from her face, but not when it's replaced by this mannequin beige, this nothingness. This is worse than death. This has never been properly alive at all.

In her daytime persona, she goes back to the murder scene. The man and his blood have been cleaned away. No stain of red or line of bright yellow police tape breaks the monotony of the grey road grey pavement grey people grey buildings grey sky.

Olivia knows then that she has to do it again. She has to see how much blood the city can drink before it leaks, before it can't swallow, before the grey is painted over everywhere.

That night, she brushes and brushes her hair until it shines and has no tangles, until she can braid it back into a tidy plait that feels like a noose in her hands. She rinses out the bloody clothes and drapes them over furniture to dry.

She stands in front of her window, staring out at the city, and cannot think of a single thing in the entire view before her that she doesn't hate.

62

Next, she tries fire.

Olivia, her face all black lines and white motley, creeps into the stillness of offices in the night. Law firms and patent companies and corporate medical organisations. All the ones she knows are to blame for the government opposing supplies for the clinic. Why give things away for free when money can be made? Why help the poor when the rich are so much more *worthwhile*, in the simplest and most mercenary sense of the term?

Their carpets spring sudden flames under the touch of her can of fuel and her lighter and then the overhead sprinkler systems kick in, leaving desks and chairs and bookshelves marked with sodden ash. The destruction calms her for a few seconds, before the rage flares up in her again.

The idea had come from the memory of a book she'd read, about Coney Island. That had been the name for an amusement park from years and years and years ago, back before the worst ages of the Wars. It had been famed for the brilliance of its lights, so bright and golden that people were dizzy from the sight.

It had been all the things that Olivia loved, once. Back when she was capable of proper feeling, of proper love. Beauty and strangeness and danger, rides and sideshows and something *different*. A place where misrule reigned.

In the end, Coney Island burned down. Those brilliant lights had been its great power, and that power had destroyed it.

Olivia likes to think that this is the optimistic version of suicidal nihilism. It's such a fitting third act to the life she's lived, poetic in its way. She remembers that first book Sam sold her, so long ago: *Dark Carnival* by Ray Bradbury.

She started with a dark carnival and now she's ending with Coney Island, burning itself down in a blaze of light brighter than any before.

63

At her job the next day, she's distracted and tired. A lifetime of habitually staying up for most of the night is catching up with her. She's irritated by the idea. Now, more than ever, she needs every hour she can wring out of a day.

In her dulled state, Olivia manages to do the classic dumb thing and spill her glass of water across her desk. Cursing under her breath, she tries to mop it up before it can do any real damage.

When her wet hand brushes against the drive port at the front of her terminal, a sharp sparking zap makes her recoil in surprise more than pain. The hard sting is gone almost as soon as it's there, but it's another few seconds before Olivia recovers from the shock of it enough to finish cleaning up the mess.

64

Next week is going to be a critical time for the project, Carabosse tells her that evening.

Donkeyskin: Ok I'll be sure to eat up all my veggies and be in fine form, then. Call me Miss Super-Spy.

You'll be here? Do you promise?

Donkeyskin: Why wouldn't I be? This isn't some game I'm gonna get bored of all of a sudden!

I didn't mean to suggest that you thought of it that way.

I merely wanted to make absolutely certain that you'd be here.

Do you promise?

Donkeyskin: Where's this sudden clinginess coming from? Yes, okay, I promise. Happy?

65

The difference between a gargoyle and a grotesque is that gargoyles are waterspouts and grotesques are just statues on buildings. The city has a lot of grotesques but not many gargoyles.

Olivia likes being on buildings and ledges where there are grotesques. She is at home among them. Another name for grotesques is chimeras. A *makara* is a chimera. Maybe she feels at home among them because she's the same. Another shadowed creepy statue, up high where nobody looks.

It's been a week since Carabosse's weird mood. She's not sure what on earth the whole "critical time for the project" thing was about, either, since her hacking work has been the same old crap as always.

'That get-up is absurd,' Sam says, instead of saying hello.

'Do you think you're a Crow now?' Hannah asks.

'It's not *a* Crow,' Olivia corrects. Hannah, of all people, should know how important nuances are when it comes to someone's mask. 'It's *the* Crow. You don't get *a* Batman, do you?'

They look taller – still not as tall as her, but taller than they were when she last saw them. Thinner, too. Otherwise they are exactly the same as in her memory, and Olivia loves them so much that it feels like the marrow in all her bones is going to burst from the force of it.

Sam makes a scoffing sound, sitting on the edge of the roof beside the grotesque. He swings his booted feet back and forth over the empty air above the street. 'Oh, so you're Batman now?'

He smiles at her. When she doesn't return it, Sam's expression falls and falters. His frown is familiar.

'I don't think Batman was the one who looked like a clown, in that story,' Hannah says quietly, standing back. She has a scar on one of her eyebrows, jagged from being unevenly stitched when fresh. Olivia wants to ask where it came from, but she doesn't want to know the answer. How many battles have they had to fight? How many times has she failed to protect them?

'Good thing for us that this isn't a story, then,' Olivia tells them.

'Yeah,' agrees Sam, staring out at the high, high drop before them. 'We know.'

66

Once she's taken her paint off, they go to Chinatown. Olivia loves Chinatown. It always reminds her of the city in *Blade Runner*: neon lights and rain. The windows of the restaurants gleam with golden chicken carcasses threaded on hooks or murky, milk-white aquariums full of half-glimpsed creatures.

This street used to make Olivia wish that she was a photographer or a writer, so that she would know the ways to capture the quickfire spitting electric beauty of it.

She doesn't wish much of anything anymore.

Getting served is always a trial for Olivia, her careful invisibility hard to shed, but Hannah and Sam are strikingly real in the cheap little dumpling shop, and it's not much time before they're ensconced in a corner table with a piled-high plate of steaming food between them.

They've brought her some paperbacks. The top of the stack is James Hilton's *Lost Horizon*. Olivia dimly remembers loving it, once, but all she thinks about as her fingers brush the cover is how many vegetables it will buy her.

She doesn't believe in Shangri-La anymore. Fairy tales are meaningless. They are too soft, too trusting. The future holds nothing but shattering disappointments.

The next book is *Fahrenheit 451* by Ray Bradbury. Olivia remembers this one, too. It's about smuggling illegal books, and about fire.

Oh, *fuck*.

They know about the fires. They probably know about the murder, too.

Guilt chokes Olivia's throat in a tight stranglehold, makes her hands shake.

'I'm sorry,' she whispers. 'I'm so fucking sorry.'

Hannah's eyes narrow. 'I don't care about them. I don't give a shit about them. They wouldn't give a shit about me. Make no mistake, they are the enemy. The Wars aren't over yet. Maybe they'll never be over. Maybe people will always find reasons to be afraid of each other. Excuses to hate.'

Hannah's words sound sincere, but Olivia doesn't buy it. Not all of it. She's pretty sure Hannah does give a shit about the people in the city.

Olivia thinks that maybe Hannah gives a shit about everyone.

The three of them have always had that in common. They care way too fucking much, and it gets them hurt time and time again.

'The reason we're giving this book to you has nothing to do with that, though,' Sam tells her. 'It's to give you a better weapon.

'When they come to you for food or cry out for protection, do more than keep them alive. Help them with living. Give them books. Paperbacks when you can afford it, digital when you can't. Give them movies, give them music.'

Olivia looks at their excited, passionate expressions and has a numb and distant gladness that Hannah wasn't the one who came to the city, that Sam is still based at the complex. Hearts like theirs wouldn't have lasted very long at all.

'It's like that story about the Beatles behind the Iron Curtain, the rib records. Don't you remember?'

She does. Distantly. It's like it happened to someone else, a long, long time ago.

Hannah is still talking, her voice hardening and growing more determined when Olivia stays unresponsive. 'It's like Saturnalia. Remember that? The feast of fools, that lords and bishops hated?

They hated it because they knew how *dangerous* it was. It was dangerous because it taught people that the ordinary way things were *wasn't the only way for them to be*. Once they knew that, they weren't going to shut up and take all the shit thrown at them anymore, were they?

'Cultures change when they have the *will* to change; and the way to give people that will is to get them *imagining*.'

67

The smog carries the whiff of meat on the stronger winds. Nothing healthy grows anywhere, except in the glassed gardens high above, which are only sharp glints of light in the soggy grey of the visible sky.

The rain is bitter on their tongues, but not poisonous enough to kill.

'Something else always gets there first,' Sam says, when Olivia remarks on the not-quite-lethal nature of the drizzle which falls on them near-constantly, wetting their hair and plastering their clothes against their skin.

They walk home to Olivia's room at dawn, when the ordinary world reclaims the streets and buildings of the city. Olivia doesn't want Hannah and Sam exposed to any more than the absolute minimum of that, if she can help it. What's the point of being a doorway guardian if you can't protect your friends from the dull horrors of grey business suits, of impatient people pushing in front of one another for the last seat on the tram?

Once they're back inside, Hannah wins the rock-paper-scissors game to decide who gets to shower the grossness of the rainwater off. Olivia and Sam sit on the floor together, their back against the wall and their knees drawn up.

'How're my chickens?'

'Fine. The small brown one–'

'Billina.'

'Yes, that one, she's still best friends with the garden rake. She stands on it and chatters whenever I'm collecting the leaves.'

Sam's words make her remember with aching clarity those

mornings in the courtyard, the chickens wandering underfoot among the vegetable rows for their brief daily freedom, while Olivia collected their eggs and cooed about what beautiful fluffy dinosaurs they were.

'One of the other ones, that bossy black one–'

'Springsteen.'

'Yeah, got sick. Hannah brought it in to live in the flat for a while. No chicken has been more babied in the history of the world. She kept saying that Springsteen wasn't allowed to die because you hadn't come back yet, so Springsteen had to hang on.'

Olivia wants to laugh out loud, even though she has a lump in her throat. 'She acts like she's such a hardass, but she's a weird sentimental goober underneath,' she says fondly, blinking several times to clear her stinging vision.

'The two of you make a matched set, then,' notes Sam. 'Because you're the opposite.'

'What do you mean?'

'You know what I mean.'

Olivia doesn't answer. Sam's never been great at metaphors, so this is probably one of those times when he hasn't really got it. There's no hard bedrock at the heart of Olivia. She's a weird sentimental goober all the way down, and if Sam truly thinks otherwise then he's in for a disappointment.

Olivia's always had a talent for disappointing people.

'God, you're such a weird idiot,' he says with an exasperated sigh. 'Don't you dare go and destroy yourself, burn yourself out to nothing, trying to hurt them, ok?'

'Reading my mind?' she jokes weakly. Sam glares in reply.

'I don't need to read your mind to know what you're thinking. Right now you are planning a gigantic turd of stinky martyr bullshit.'

'That's one way to phrase it. A unique and scatological way,' she says, trying to maintain jollity and failing.

'This was never meant to be a permanent thing. When you've got the complex hidden away in a made-up poison zone, then you get out of this city and you don't look back, ok? I wouldn't have let you go in the first place if it meant you weren't ever coming home.'

'You kicked up a big stink about it; I'd hardly call that *letting* me. Which, *wow*, is pretty paternalistic and gross as far as phrasing goes, *jackass*. I didn't need your *permission* to give up everything remotely good and happy in my life,' she tries to snap angrily, but the words come out wavery and plaintive and she feels like a dumb crybaby. She blinks hard until her vision clears, then wipes her cheeks and stares at Sam defiantly.

'This wasn't meant to be a permanent solution,' Sam says again, his voice even. 'If you need to come home now, and we can't make the map plan work, then we'll find other ways. We weren't ever going to be able to hide entirely, not forever. What you've done here has been incredibly important: it gave us the time to plan, to gather supplies to protect ourselves in the long run.

'We've got enough weapons and ammunition stockpiled to defend the complex against a decade's worth of attacks, if it came to that, and frankly we aren't worth the time and trouble for anyone to bother trying *that* hard to get rid of us. Why would a development party risk a violent skirmish for a piece of land no better than any other, when there are so many zones with nobody in them at all? They'll leave us alone. Everyone wins that way. And the ones who do bother us-'

'We can use the guns on,' Olivia finishes for him. Sam rolls his eyes.

'You and Hannah are way too bloodthirsty for your own goods, holy shit. The guns are there as *insurance*, you psycho. In the best case scenario, they'll never get used.

'If a development team comes along I'm gonna give them *jam*. And peanut butter. And tomatoes and pumpkins and whatever else we've got handy. You'd know as well as anyone how hard it is to come by anything properly edible in the city. How else do you think I managed to survive a thrive childhood, except by learning how to bribe people with food? You'd be amazed what people will do for something nice to eat.

'Come back with us now.' Sam's voice turns soft, pleading. 'We'll manage. It'll be all right.'

'No. I'm going to see it through,' Olivia shakes her head. 'It's only a few more months.'

'Can you last that much longer, though?'

Instead of answering, Olivia stands up, looks at the lightening sky out the window. 'I'd better get ready for work.'

She takes her makeup into the bathroom, where Hannah is drying her hair.

'This stuff always seemed so effortless for my mother,' Olivia confesses as she opens her cosmetics bag. 'She wore it like it made her feel better.'

Hannah reaches up, rubbing her thumb against a cut on Olivia's forehead.

'I was in a fight in the evening. Before you got to me,' Olivia explains.

'It'll get infected if you don't clean it better than this,' Hannah warns.

'Sorry,' Olivia says. She's been saying that a lot since Hannah and Sam showed up.

Hannah reaches into the recesses of her jacket and pulls out a tiny first aid kit. 'Sit. Up on the counter.'

Without waiting to check that Olivia will follow the order – Olivia does, too cowed to think of doing otherwise – Hannah opens the kit and spreads its contents on the counter beside Olivia.

The alcoholic swab is cool and sharply burning all at once as Hannah wipes it over Olivia's forehead. It stings, but Olivia doesn't care because when Hannah brings the swab away it's smeared with the vile gloop that Olivia wears as foundation, that she put on before they went out to dinner.

Hannah is stripping away the mask that freezes Olivia's face through all the long and lonely days, digging the girl that Olivia used to be out from under the rubble.

'This is deep,' Hannah notes, continuing her work with a

second swab. 'There's maybe going to be a scar. Don't think I haven't noticed these other two scars here on your cheek, either. Fuck you, how many times did I fucking tell you not to work with Carabosse, you fucking idiot.'

Beneath the layer of foundation still on most of her face, Olivia can feel the warm flush of shame on her cheeks. She can't remember the last time she cared enough about anything to feel ashamed. She gulps back a laugh that bubbles like tar in her throat.

'Please, please, try to remember.' Hannah's voice is even and quiet as she continues her meticulous work. 'That the first duty of a revolutionary is to survive.'

68

It rains in earnest, the kind of downpour that gets exposure level warnings on the news, just before Olivia heads out to work. She looks at the torrent of poisons coming down, and the flimsy umbrella that'll leave her legs soaked no matter what.

'Screw it. I hate that job anyway,' she says, and closes the door again. 'Plug that kettle into the wall there. I've got some soup sachets here somewhere.'

They sit on the bed in a row, their legs covered by Olivia's blanket, and sip their artificial tomato broth.

'The girl showed up yesterday morning, on a bicycle. I don't know how far she rode on it, but she was pretty chipper, so I guess she didn't have much trouble on the way,' Hannah tells Olivia. 'Her name's Winter. I don't know if that's her real name or the handle she picked for herself. Not that it matters one way or the other. She said she had a message from Carabosse for me and Sam, that we had to come to the city and see you ASAP.'

'Really?' Olivia's so surprised that she forgets to sip her soup carefully, and burns her tongue.

'Jesse came too, though he decided to stay out of the main city for now,' Hannah goes on. 'He says he needs to get used to it before he's ready for the full-volume experience. Eric's out at the complex, but he's doing okay too. I think they needed some time apart from each other.'

Olivia feels terrible for Jesse and Eric, pushed away from one another by the ghost that's always between them now. She feels so grateful, and so selfish, to be sitting here with Hannah and Sam, all of them alive, all of them drinking gross artificial soup from chipped cups and listening to the icy drum of rain against the windows.

And she feels unhappy for herself, too, because it seems cruel and unfair that she's given up so much and worked so hard to protect the complex, and yet she can't protect the people there from sorrows, from change.

Even if she makes it back there someday, it won't be the same as it was when she left. Jesse will be gone. Maybe Esperanza's found someone else she wants to kiss, more than she wants to kiss Olivia.

Olivia still hasn't told Carabosse that Ariette's dead. The longer she leaves it, the more impossible it is to bring it up.

'There are new people. You'll like them,' Hannah goes on brightly. 'Haydar can't use his legs, so he's been doing the laundry and sorting out the library, things he can do from his chair. Now there's Winter, too, I guess. She'll probably work in the garden and on gathering trips with me, like Ariette did. Or maybe she's nothing like Ariette. I didn't get a chance to hang with her before we left to come here.'

'They sound nice,' Olivia agrees, stumped for words. She can't imagine ever getting the chance to meet those new people, much less having a life that intersects with theirs. 'What about you two? What are you up to lately?'

Sam and Hannah exchange a look, and Sam shakes his head. 'You're going to have to see for yourself when you come home.'

'I think I met Winter a couple of times,' Olivia says, deflecting the conversation away from thoughts of her going home. 'Working on the zoning stuff. It's nice she gets to pay that hard work off by seeing the complex.'

'There's no point in saving everyone else if you don't save yourself.' Sam's voice is flat. He frowns at her. 'We don't want to be saved if it's without you. You're part of the world that deserves protecting, idiot.'

'Yeah, yeah. How long can you two stay?'

'Not long. We should go once the rain clears. Please come back with us.'

Olivia swallows hard, waiting a few seconds before she trusts her voice to stay level as she speaks. 'No. I need to see this through.'

'You have to promise to look after yourself better,' Hannah insists. 'When goddamn *Satan*... sorry, I mean *Carabosse*, is worried about you, that's a signal that it's time to make some lifestyle changes.'

After that they stop talking about serious, important things, and just enjoy each other's company. Olivia's never thought of herself as an especially physical person – the Capoeira and the face-painting are the only times she's ever really been conscious of herself as a *body*, rather than as a brain that can move around – but there's a comfort in having Sam and Hannah close by that's so tangible and real that it makes her eyes prickle with tears.

All too soon, it's time for them to go. Olivia hugs them tight, as if she can engrave their molecules into her own skin by clinging on hard enough.

'You come home soon, and come home safe, all right?' Hannah demands, clutching Olivia just as tightly, 'Or I'll make you wish you'd never shared that rice and gravy with the kid in the rabbit mask.'

That earns a snuffly laugh from Olivia. She presses her forehead to Hannah's. 'You say that like I don't regret it every day.'

Then it's Sam's turn. Olivia cups his scarred, half-curled hand in both her own gently, wishing that she could warm the damage away by sheer force of the love she has for him.

'Don't forget to share the books,' he tells her. 'Remember what Plutarch said. "The mind is not a vessel to be filled but a fire to be kindled". If you give people knowledge, that's going to end up capable of way more damage than setting off sprinkler systems in offices.'

'I guess that was kind of dumb,' she replies, embarrassed. Sam shakes his head.

'Not dumb. Desperate. I get it, trust me,' he assures her.

It's not often that Sam's the one to initiate hugs between them, but he does this time, and Olivia hugs back with all her might.

69

Donkeyskin: You're such a dork. I can't believe you were freaking out about me so much you called in the cavalry.

I felt obligated to take responsibility for your wellbeing.

I'd been so pleased to see the work you were doing as the Candy Butcher that I hadn't considered how much stress you were under.

How sad you were.

And when the full extent of your situation became clear to me, I feared I was too late to help.

Donkeyskin: Dorrrrrrrrk.

It wouldn't have come to this if you'd talked honestly to me about how you were feeling from the start.

Donkeyskin: Yeah because you're a big sharer.

Donkeyskin: Always volunteering personal information, that's you.

Sarcasm doesn't translate into the written medium very elegantly, you know. Either it's too subtle to be detected, or it's so obvious as to be crass.

Donkeyskin: I was too subtle right

Yes. That's exactly what the problem was.

Donkeyskin: Whereas that, right there, was really obvious. No points for you.

Donkeyskin: That Winter girl, I met her once, right? She was the peppy one with mad RFID skills.

Yes. That's her.

I choose someone likely to be a good fit for what I know about the complex.

Winter is about as different from Arachne as it's possible for two young people to be without being on opposing sides ideologically, but each had something that suited what I know of the place you have there.

And while we're on the subject, I know about Arachne's death. You don't have to keep trying to avoid telling me.

Donkeyskin: It was awful.

Donkeyskin: It was so awful.

Donkeyskin: I liked her. I think we were friends.

Donkeyskin: The thing I keep thinking about, over and over, is how differently it might have all gone if there weren't the pulses.

Donkeyskin: Even if she'd been hurt, if we'd been able to contact each other, then we could have driven out and picked them all up. Treated Ariette and Sam's injuries right away, instead of them having to stumble home bleeding.

Donkeyskin: We could have had a network with all the others around us, to pool knowledge and resources. There might have been someone nearby with better medical training than a bunch of shitty frightened kids.

Donkeyskin: The complex gets by fine for day to day stuff, but the isolation is how they kill us. It's not only the violence. That's just the obvious way. Ariette died because they stop us from banding together effectively.

Donkeyskin: That's why I'm here. That's what I want to accomplish. I want to buy the zone around the complex enough safety, enough calm, that they

Donkeyskin: that WE can begin to find a way to fight back. To find the source of the pulses and put it out of commission. To give us as good a chance as anyone else to band together and survive.

I will do whatever I can to help you.

I hate the pulses more than you can imagine.

Donkeyskin: Look at us and our long-term goal-making.

Donkeyskin: Guess I'm going to have to survive this whole stupid adventure after all.

Looks like it, yeah.

70

She photocopies her favourite poems and passages from the books in her possession, and pastes them up the same way she does the medical information sheets. Tiny slivers of imagination scattered across the city like seeds.

Olivia's got no idea if anybody's going to read them or think they're interesting. She has to try, though, even if she has no certainty about what'll happen next.

For Ariette, as a final good-bye, she finds an old wood carving of a spider in its web in an art book. She photocopies it and then, below the picture, Olivia carefully copies out a quote that she hopes Ariette would have approved of.

I used to think I was the strangest person in the world but then I thought there are so many people in the world, there must be someone just like me who feels bizarre and flawed in the same ways I do. I would imagine her, and imagine that she must be out there thinking of me too. Well, I hope that if you are out there and read this and know that, yes, it's true I'm here, and I'm just as strange as you.

– Frida Kahlo

She pastes the copies high up on buildings, on the edges of their rooftop, so that the sun will strike the words on those rare occasions when the clouds open at all.

71

She finds a new day job to fill her hours and her bank account, behind the reception desk of a large dental practice. The work isn't especially different to the administration tasks she had at the bank, or even those from her long-ago days on the computer level of the factory.

As simple as it is, the job allows her to meet a lot of new people every day. Among so many polite smiles and small-talk exchanges, it's hard for her to feel as alone as she used to. By the end of her shifts, she is glad to be going home to her own company for a few hours, before the other half of her routine starts after sundown.

Her hair gets longer and she dyes it blue-black, claiming her appearance back bit by bit from the anonymity that swallowed her like quicksand. She gets a gold stud in her nose, and then takes it out again after a couple of weeks because it makes using tissues even more difficult than the face-paint does. Olivia almost always has a cold or sniffle or cough to contend with these days. The pollution's getting worse, and she isn't sleeping enough each night for her immune system to be that great.

To help her battered lungs get stronger, she jogs after work. Her new job is in a rich enough part of town that there's a park not far from the dentist's office. Children often play there in the evenings under the watchful eyes of their parents.

When she hears those kids laughing and shrieking and calling out to each other, it's easier for her to remember that the city is, for huge swathes of its population, a wonderful utopia. Any problems it has are seen as small problems, not worth worrying about.

She wonders how on earth anyone could be so blinkered. Do they think of it at all, while they enjoy the twilight? Do they think of the people who have almost nothing and have to fight for every inch of what they have?

Are these people watching their children in the late sunlight frightened of those others, the ones surviving in the dark?

Olivia hopes so. She hopes they're terrified. She hopes it keeps them up at night. Nobody deserves to sleep easily in a comfortable bed while things are as they are.

Her own nightmares are as bad as they ever were, but sometimes she has good dreams too. She dreams of Sam's tiny room, with the smells from the souvlaki kitchen downstairs seeping up warm and laden with garlic, and the strewn piles of soft discarded clothes on his floor.

She dreams of Hannah in a red rabbit mask, bringing her a pile of care-worn paperback books and little trays of food.

She dreams of the carving around the door to their home, salvaged from a forgotten museum and given a new chance to be seen and loved.

She reads books on Buddhism and finds them more comforting than she expected. She downloads the first one on a whim, wondering if it will contain any secrets on how to deal with the empty space inside herself. The books are sanctioned texts, so the information is a rudimentary overview at best, but it's a comfort.

She begins to feel that she's come back to herself, back to being Olivia.

That self has changed in the meantime, of course. That was unavoidable. Some of her edges are harder, and her laugh has a catch in it. But that's all right. Changing is proof that she's alive, and she is very grateful to be that.

72

As good as her soup-making skills are and as nourishing as the results tend to be, Olivia tries to shake it up a bit. She remembers that stale crappy popcorn she'd bought so eagerly at the factory. People have other kinds of hungers and need other kinds of feeding.

It'd be stupid for her to be nicknamed the Candy Butcher if she never has any candy to offer.

Caramels and rock lollipops aren't much more complicated than powdered soup to make, so Olivia puts those together first. She remembers eating candied fruit as a child, how special it always was as a treat, but decides that's going to have to wait – for the time being, any fruit that comes her way gets passed on to hungry people in its fresh form, to preserve whatever vitamins are present.

One night she's painted up as Pierrot, dishing out daal stew as the main meal and shards of dark brittle toffee as a treat for those who want it. As usual, someone else has brought bread along, and there's a lemony cordial to drink that masks most of the bitter flavour of the water. Everyone's in good spirits, or at least feeling better than they were.

A boy and a girl make their way to the head of the queue. They look about twelve or thirteen, the boy a little older than the girl, but it's hard to be certain because their faces are decorated with painted domino masks – peacock blue for her, rusty oxblood red for him.

'Do you want to help me ladle it out?' Olivia asks. The girl nods decisively, and takes over from Olivia at the stew pot. The boy passes bread to those who already have their bowl or plate filled.

'I'm Carve,' he tells Olivia. 'She's Etch.'

'Nice to meet you.'

The three of them work together until all the food is handed out. During that time, Olivia notices details about the pair: how Carve's body language is tuned to keep Etch in his line of sight as much as possible, the way both of them wear shirts with high collars and sleeves with holes cut for their thumbs, so the cuff can be pulled right down to their fingers.

'You came to the clinic,' Olivia realises. She never bothers to compartmentalise her identity down here in the thrive slums. These aren't the people she needs to stay hidden from.

'Immunosuppressants,' Etch agrees with a nod, equally forthright with information that, in other company, she would hold back.

It's not that the thrive slums are safe, per se – the resources are scarce enough that many of the residents here will exploit any weakness they find in others, simply to increase the chances that they'll survive themselves – but rather that, for Olivia at least, to be honest seems the lesser of two battles.

She remembers the pair, now. They'd been much less healthy looking the last time she'd seen them, and they're hardly the picture of robust good cheer now. Skinny, dirty, stitches and grafts still healing all over their bodies where veins or skin had been extracted in hurried procedures.

They'd been economical with their words then, too. The boy had walked up to where Olivia sat behind the waiting-room counter, leaving the girl to perch on the edge of one of the plastic chairs that lined the small area.

'I have a fake liver. She's got fake lungs and a fake heart,' he'd said. 'We need the stuff that makes them stick.'

Clearly their grasp on the terminology has evolved since then. They weren't the first test subjects Olivia met working at the clinic, but they'd been the youngest. There was no way on earth they were old enough to consent to artificial organ trials or the donation of their original organs that went along with it.

Legally, porting was the only commercial medical procedure that minors could undergo, but everyone knew that nobody cared what happened to thrive kids. They were worth far more in pieces. Probably the only reason these two had managed to negotiate inclusion an artificial trial in addition to the donations was because they had each other to fight for as well as themselves.

'You're both looking well,' Olivia says to them now. Carve gives her a quick smile.

'That stuff you got for us made the difference.'

'I doubt that. I mean, thanks for the thought, but I only managed to find that one week's worth of doses for you both.'

'No, no. Not like that. There are heaps of ways to get medicine. But you gave a shit about whether we lived or died.'

'That's a rarity,' Etch adds in her own quiet voice.

Olivia's brow furrows, always an odd sensation when she does it while wearing her paint. 'Don't you get any ongoing care, as part of the artificial organ trial?'

'Nah.' Carve shakes his head. 'All they needed from us was to see if the things would take. Once we woke up and didn't drop dead, they had what they needed. Any complications that show up later, they can treat in the people who pay for the parts instead of getting them free.'

Olivia doesn't know why things like this still shock and surprise her. She should be used to hearing these things by now.

She is grateful that she still has the capacity to be horrified, though. She hopes tragedy never seems unremarkable to her.

After they're done serving out the food, the pair linger close to her. Eventually, Etch clears her throat, looking nervous.

'Can we… we were wondering, can we put up fliers like yours? With stories and poems, and information that people might need?'

'Are you asking me for *permission*?' Olivia asks, laughing. 'I'm not boss of the walls, guys. Put up whatever you like.'

The words seem to baffle the pair. 'Really?'

'Yeah. Make your own truth.' She thinks, suddenly, of the black-lit wall of the club. *Love is a Virus*. 'Maybe you'll inspire someone else in turn, and it'll spread out and out.'

'I wish I could do the other things you do,' Etch sighs. From the way her fists curl and uncurl at her sides as she speaks, Olivia knows what other things she means.

'Did,' she corrects. 'I don't now. It didn't fix anything. It didn't make me feel better. It just put more hurt into the world.'

'At least we weren't the ones getting hurt, for a change.'

Olivia shrugs. 'I'm not gonna spin you some abyss-gazes-into-you shit. Like I said, I can't give you permission or forbid you or anything. I'm no role model one way or the other. But I don't do it anymore. Not the fires, not the killing. Take from that whatever you want.'

73

Operation Chess Fortress is approximately 92.4% complete.

Donkeyskin: That's a very specific approximate. Are you sure you know what that word even means?

Considering I only went to one decimal place, I'd say I demonstrated adequate knowledge of the term, yes.

Donkeyskin: "Operation Chess Fortress" huh

Donkeyskin: Remember that time you accused *me* of being a drama queen?

I believe I said you had a flair for the theatrical.

Donkeyskin: You sure are in a splitting-hairs kind of mood today that's for sure

Donkeyskin: I like the name though. Very apt. Cute.

I thought you might.

Donkeyskin: Your creepily comprehensive knowledge of my past isn't nearly as endearing as you think it is.

Donkeyskin: More importantly holy shit are you serious.

Donkeyskin: We're that close to the end? Really?

Yes.

74

Carve and Etch have made their home in a factory warehouse with an interior almost entirely composed of rubble. What structural integrity remains seems more reliant on luck than anything else, but despite the shaky conditions, seventeen thrive kids and other young exiles are bedding down there.

Olivia wishes she could scoop them all up and bring them out to the complex, but the best she can do is tell them what life is like out past the margins of the cities. Some of them look interested, but others wrinkle their noses in distaste at the descriptions of vegetable gardens and endless ruins.

It makes Olivia smile to see the diversity of reactions. Town mice and country mice are who they are, no matter where she finds them.

She teaches them the games she used to play with Jesse and Ariette and Eric when they were teaching her how to move, *Gato Doente* and Mister Wolf and Statues, by the light of generator-bulbs and candles. The hollowed-out space inside the warehouse is more than large enough for chasing games. Their shadows on the walls are huge and quick-changing.

The kids are close to silent, despite their obvious excitement and enjoyment, and their skills at avoiding capture are almost supernatural. They've done it often enough in the real world, for stakes far higher than winning a game.

Etch gets exhausted after a while, and comes to sit beside Olivia on the edge of the impromptu playing field.

'Ever heard of a chess fortress?' Olivia asks her.

Etch shakes her head. 'I've barely heard of chess, to be honest.'

Olivia smiles at that. 'A friend reminded me about chess fortresses the other day. I'd forgotten. It's this way to break a game, basically. Computers used to crash if you tried it when you played against them. They didn't have any programming to deal with a player who didn't give a shit about conquering the board, who only cared about protecting their own pieces.

'Obviously that isn't the case anymore, with computers. They get it now, but it took a long time for them to learn.

'A chess fortress is where one side sets up a barrier around their king. It makes a thing called a passive draw, and that ends the game. There's no way for the attacking side to break through and win. So long as the fortress-builder doesn't change their mind and decide to go after the other king, the game will stay in stasis forever.

'When you build a chess fortress, you're basically hacking the system. Refusing to play. That's all the complex has ever tried to do. We just wanted to stay where we were, living the way we wanted.'

'No.' Etch shakes her head. 'If that were true, you wouldn't have done those things that you disown now. You'd love to see them lose their king someday. You know you would.'

'Maybe. I'm not certain. I think nonviolence is more effective in the long run. It's harder to use love and art, but they work in a way that I haven't ever seen destruction or deprivation work.'

Etch snorts. 'Please. Love never saved anyone.'

'In my experience, it's the only thing that ever does,' Olivia answers quietly.

75

Jesse moves into a place not far out from the inner city, and gets a job making coffees for the early morning rush of workers spilling out of trains and car parks every day.

'They like my hair,' he tells Olivia. 'You'd be surprised how many of them think it's cool. No, really! They don't want to be like this themselves, but that doesn't mean they don't like knowing that somebody else is, out in the world, you know?'

Olivia shrugs. She doesn't know half as much as she used to, especially not about the people in the city. She thinks everyone needs to stop assuming they know anything about what people who are different to them are like. Then they'd see that the thrives weren't less than them, the people outside the city weren't less than them, the people poorer than them, the maskers, the hungry kids, everyone. All different but all equal, all important.

She suspects Jesse would say "well, yeah, *duh*" if she articulated any of that, though, so she sticks with a shrug, and helps him get the cups and milk and sugar ready for the oncoming tide of customers.

She likes being out first-thing in the morning – or last-thing, if she's been out all night with Etch and Carve – and seeing the world as it shifts from night to day with weak dawn light. Everything always feels exciting then.

Going to work is usually a last-thing for Jesse, too. After his shift ends he sleeps through the rest of the day and wakes up in the evening. He's in a band, and they suck, but Olivia thinks they have more fun that way. The audiences at the parties and dives and shitty clubs they play in don't seem to mind that they suck. They're noisy and energetic and Jesse has a charismatic smile. Entire rock and roll careers have been built on less.

'This first song is about a guy I know with a fucked-up hand. I don't gotta tell you how he got it – most of you probably know a guy of your own with a fucked-up hand, or a girl with a big scar on her face, or you used to have a sister but you don't now, or whatever. That's not what this song's about. I got enough songs about that shit already.

'This is about that guy, and how he's an architect, drawing designs for houses and shit. He mostly hates having to talk to people, but since he can't draw himself he's gotta tell other people what to put down, right. You do what you gotta, if you believe in the outcome enough.

'So this song's for him, and for everyone who's tired of living in ruins. It's called *Building With Our Broken Hands*.'

76

Now that she's got Carve and Etch there to help her get everything home when she's finished, Olivia plans a trip to one of the bigger, better-stocked supermarkets. The one near her room never has much of anything, but going further out in search of better supplies requires more time, energy and logistics than she's had at her disposal.

The supermarket three blocks from the dentist's office where she works is so different to the one near where she lives that it seems a cruel satire to call them by the same title. Instead of grubby wire shelves of battered, off-brand things that're more chemical than food, this supermarket is gleaming, so bright that Olivia half expects all the shoppers around her to don sunglasses against the glare.

It has a salad bar, for crying out loud, stainless-steel dishes of fresh-chopped fruit resting on a trough of ice so shoppers can pick and choose how much watermelon they want in their mix as opposed to honeydew.

Olivia wonders why the writers of the novels she loves bothered making up triffids and Pennywise the clown and the Cyclops, when the real world already has fake ambulances for skipping traffic and overcrowded factory dormitories so cold that kids run up and down in loading docks until they've stopped shivering enough that they can sleep, when there are luxurious salad bars in the supermarkets of good neighbourhoods and nothing to eat at all in the bad ones.

Maybe the writers knew that without the creatures and the monsters and the made-up things thrown in, the other things are too much to bear. Reality without an edge of imagination is too much like despair without hope.

They split up. Etch goes to see what meats would be the smartest purchase, Carve commandeers the vegetables and beans, and Olivia seeks out flour and sugar, dried pasta and noodles, and spices.

She's got a packet of fusilli in one hand and one of rotini in the other, idling over making a choice simply because it's the most useless thing she can imagine doing (little spirals or little spirals? How can she decide?!) and that makes it kind of fun. It's nice to be presented with the absurdity of existence and be amused by it, rather than exhausted, once in a while.

Olivia's looking from one package of pasta to the other and then she notices how *quiet* it is. People are still listening to headphones as they push their trolleys down the aisles, or talking to one another, or dropping tins and making unexpected sharp noises. But behind that stuff, everything's gone silent. There's no soft music getting piped in, no air conditioner, no beeps of bar-code readers as shopping gets bought, no humming drone of the frozen and chilled food section maintaining its temperature.

Her feet are moving before her brain has finished processing all the signals into a coherent reaction. The deli-meat counter is several aisles away, but she makes it there and crouches behind what little cover it affords before the overhead address system crackles back into life.

'We're sorry to interrupt your afternoon, shoppers,' the cheerful voice says brightly. 'This won't take long, it's a standard security check, nothing to be worried about.'

Fuck. *Fuck*. She can't believe she thought she could pull this off.

When she'd looked like someone who belonged in this neighbourhood, when she was a kid, she'd thought that all it took to convince people that you belonged somewhere was confidence. If you looked like you knew where you were going, nobody stopped you.

Now she knows it's not that simple. She's got scars on her face that haven't been modded away, or convincingly covered with makeup. Her clothes are inexpensive, shapeless and a little faded. Etch and Carve blend in no better than she does. Of *course* they've been noticed.

For fuck's sake, Olivia has actual money in her pocket – some of it in coins! How did she think they were ever going to get away with being here, where every single other shopper was paying with the wave of a chip?

Carve arrives behind the counter a few seconds after she does. They can see Etch on the other side of the deli area, crouched in an awkward corner-space between two display tables. She catches their eyes and gives them a nod, as if to say *I'm okay*.

Which is bullshit, of course. None of them are okay.

'Stay where you are,' the happy overhead voice goes on. 'While the team comes around and checks your ID. It'll only take a minute.'

'We're not doing anything illegal,' Carve says under his breath. 'There's no *law* that says we can't shop here... is there?'

Olivia shakes her head. 'No. But they aren't *arresting* anyone, are they? They'll just be *interested*. Maybe they'll run a background check to see who we are. If we might like to go to a more convenient store closer to home.'

'We'll be fine,' Carve tries to assure her. 'It'll be their usual standover shit, a bit of bullying to put us in our place. It's nothing. It's fine.'

But Olivia's been at this long enough to know better than that. 'It's enough to get us flagged. Anything we do, anywhere we go, will be recorded and cross-referenced.'

They can't afford that. They can't let their faces, the names they go by in everyday life, become especial targets for scrutiny. Even without their nightly activities, surviving in the darker tiers of the city means breaking a thousand petty rules every day. It's impossible to get by otherwise, except by pushing the law to its limits and then a bit over. Water rations, curfews –

who knows which of these will be the thing that gets them called up for a quick chat with the authorities? Nobody knows where they wind up, the ones who get noticed. Olivia's got a vivid imagination about the possibilities.

Right now, best case scenario, the three of them have a life expectancy of maybe a week.

Olivia always knew this might happen. She feels so sorry for Sam and Hannah. She wishes she could tell them that she loves them. She wishes she could take away the sadness they'll feel when she never comes home.

It's fucking hilarious. She's a vigilante, a murderer, a vandal, and in the end she's going to wind up dead over groceries.

She's given away an aching, bloodied portion of herself to working on the chess fortress, on protecting her home. The levels of treason involved are the stuff of crime novels and action movies. She's a fucking *spy*, for crying out loud.

And in the end all her plans came to nothing, because she wanted to go to a supermarket with fancy pasta.

She hopes, desperately, that Carabosse and the others can finish without her.

Olivia glances at Carve beside her, and Etch a short distance further away. They look how she feels: resolute, resigned. Like they always expected that things would end up like this for them, one way or another.

She tries to tell herself that she has no duty of care towards them. That she's no role model, no hero, and they're no sidekicks. They are themselves, and they've made their own choices, and they'd hate it if they knew she was thinking about them so protectively, as though she has some responsibility towards them.

But she does. She needs to save them. She doesn't care if they get pissed off at her for her dumb, weird maternal feelings. In fact, she desperately hopes they do. Right now, Olivia wants nothing more than for the two of them to live long enough to be annoyed at her.

For the first time in a long time, she thinks of her own parents. She remembers how, when she was a kid, she'd been afraid that somebody would find out that she'd been reading *Donkeyskin* and infer things about her father, ruin his reputation.

That old nightmare's going to finally come true, a thousand times worse than she ever imagined it. Her parents' lives will be ruined. Soon enough someone's going to take her fingerprints or scan her face, and bring up her identity on a computer somewhere, and-

The idea forms in her head like the world coming into focus in front of her glasses.

'Are either of you ported?' she asks Etch and Carve quietly. Their arms are so marked with other scars that she never noticed one way or another if they had the more common damage, too.

'I am,' Carve replies under his breath. 'Why?'

'There might be a way for us to get out of this.' Olivia glances around until she finds the magnetic strip attached to the counter, holding various knives in place. She sends up a quick hope to a universe she doubts is paying attention that there won't be anything really bad on the blade, since Carve's on immunosuppressants and could do without new and exciting bacteria in his bloodstream.

She slices a long, shallow cut into her own palm first, working her fingers open and closed quickly to get the blood up to the air in the wound. Carve holds his own hand out to her without hesitation or question, and Olivia really, really hopes that this isn't the stupidest and most useless thing she's ever tried.

Carve winces as she flicks the knife over his skin, then mimics her gesture to make the gash bleed quickly. While he's doing that, Olivia looks to Etch, who gives her a nod. This one, Olivia knows, means *I'll follow*.

If they had a battery charger, or a battery itself, Olivia would be more confident in this idea. Well, no. It's a ridiculous long shot no matter what. She tells herself that it wouldn't make a difference either way.

Still, it'd be nice to have more than her own blood and a good hunch to work with.

Oh well, too late now.

She presses her bleeding palm against Carve's, the liquids slipping and mingling together over their skin as they interlace their fingers, linking the circuits of their systems together as Olivia shuts her eyes and thinks, with all her might and as loudly as she can:

CARABOSSE!

77

When Olivia was a little kid, before any of the important things in her life had happened, she and her parents went on a trip to the ocean. The real ocean, the kind in story books, the kind that people could swim in.

The moment she remembers most from that holiday is of a real wave crashing into her. It hadn't been like in the tide pools back home. That much force, all at once, without any regulation keeping it in check, had been hard. Like a slap. It had knocked her feet out from under her.

As the onslaught of raw data hits her, Olivia's only thought is *Hannah and Sam always knew about the ocean after all.*

It only lasts for a second before it abates, leaving her heart hammering in her chest and her brain feeling like her ears do after a really loud sound. Carve makes a grunt of surprise beside her, his hand clenching against her own.

The roar is still there, but at a distance – the difference between being tossed by an undertow and standing on a shore in a storm. She has enough time to feel relief at the lessened pressure in her head before every light in the place goes black, save for a single dimmed exit sign in the wall at the end of the homewares aisle.

They run. Olivia and Carve are almost dragging one another, lurching forward as fast as they're able while keeping their hands joined. Etch, moving alone, is faster, and gets there first. She kicks someone aside in the near-total darkness and the person makes an "oomph" sound as they fall back hard.

Etch gets the door open just as Carve and Olivia catch up with her and they're out and slamming the door behind them, sealing the rest of the supermarket patrons and the security personnel temporarily in darkness.

The afternoon is overcast but Olivia's eyes dance with spots from the abrupt transition from light to dark to light. Or the spots are a residual effect from her mind being hit by an invisible truck.

Either way, it's Etch who stays the vital half-step faster than the two still bleeding. 'There.'

She's pointing at a building on the other side of the street. It's the kind that has levels devoted to all different sorts of uses, with a high-end furniture display store on the ground floor. The store's fire alarms are activated. The lights inside flash on and off and a loud beeping pattern screams out.

Customers are filing out of the doors, mixed with the tenants and office workers from higher floors coming down the internal staircase.

'Wait, no, there,' Etch corrects herself, disregarding the cacophony of distraction and moving instead towards another blinking light, this one coming from a paper supply store window beside a flight of stairs leading down to an underground train station.

They swipe their transit cards at the turnstile and make their way down the stairs to the platform, on legs shaking so hard that Olivia leans on the handrail like it's all she has left. It takes everything in them to go at an ordinary pace when they want to keep running, to get as far away from their brush with a stupid, easy, pointless end.

It's not until they're two stations away from the platform, the three of them standing and swaying in the crush of commuters like anyone else, that Olivia and Carve let go of each other's hands. The blanket of mental silence that immediately falls over Olivia, leaving her alone with nobody's thought-noise but her own, makes her sag in relief.

Maybe one day she'll feel that deep soul-loneliness again. Probably. Almost certainly, since she's pretty sure it's fundamental to the human condition or whatever.

But for now, Olivia is very glad to be on her own in her brain.

78

Where are you now?

Donkeyskin: You mean you can't tell?

I count fourteen proxies on your session, and have enough faith in your ability to assume that there are at least several more I have yet to detect.

So no. I can't tell.

Donkeyskin: You've only found fourteen, seriously?

Donkeyskin: If I'd known your game was that weak I would have worked out another way to get out of there.

Donkeyskin: We're somewhere safe. We're all feeling kind of stupid and shaken up, but we're safe.

Donkeyskin: Once it's nightfall we'll head home.

It isn't your home.

Donkeyskin: Well no

Donkeyskin: Not if you want to get super literal about it

Donkeyskin: it's a figure of speech

Donkeyskin: This? This is what you want to talk about, now of all times? My need to get out of the city before it breaks me?

Donkeyskin: Trust me I know that already. Today has been a fairly pointed reminder of how much I don't want to be here.

Donkeyskin: And as soon as chess fortress is done I'll go

No.

There's very little left to do. I'm more than capable of handling it on my own.

In truth I could have been doing so for at least the last week, perhaps two. It was selfishness that stopped me from saying so.

I didn't want you to leave.

That almost cost you your life today.

Donkeyskin: Oh please, today's bullshit is entirely on me. I wanted to go to a fancy supermarket. That isn't your fault.

Donkeyskin: I mean, leaving aside the part where you saved us, which was badass.

Donkeyskin: What if you'd told me to go two weeks ago and I had and then I'd been killed by a dumb accident or something?

Donkeyskin: A crumbling house. What if a crumbling house had fallen on me? You'd have been like, well shit, that sure is my fault for telling her to go.

Donkeyskin: Look at the disaster you saved me from.

Olivia.

Donkeyskin: Hey come on I'm using twenty proxies here. Do you have any idea how bad form it is to use my real name when I'm being careful like this? RUDE.

Olivia, I know the thought of going home frightens you.

But once you stop being frightened, think how wonderful you'll feel.

Donkeyskin: nah pretty much still just feeling frightened

Donkeyskin: I'm so fucked up now. I've done awful things.

You've done good things, too.

Donkeyskin: what if i don't fit with them like before

Then you'll find a new way to fit with them.

Donkeyskin doesn't stay Donkeyskin at the end of the story, does she?

There comes a time when you have to put aside the disguise, and be the person under it.

Whoever she may be.

Donkeyskin: And Carabosse stays Carabosse at the end of that story.

Donkeyskin: I'm really glad you were there to help today.

How did you know I would be?

Donkeyskin: "Know" is a strong word. More like "hoped", if that.

Donkeyskin: But I knew you kept an alert set up for me. I worked that out after you freaked out over me being depressed, and got red rabbit and robot mouse

Donkeyskin: (SEE HOW EASY IT IS TO CALL PEOPLE THINGS THAT AREN'T THEIR REAL NAMES?)

Donkeyskin: to come check up on me.

Donkeyskin: You only found out I was sad because I got that shock from the computer.

Donkeyskin: If Sam hadn't shown me what it felt like, back when we were kids, you wouldn't have known me.

You just used his real name.

Donkeyskin: fuck you

Donkeyskin: I'm trying to have a sincere moment of gratitude here, and show you how I knew it'd work – which you asked me, so I'm being polite and answering your question!!! – and you can't stop ruining everything by being a jackass.

Donkeyskin: I worked out who you are, though.

Donkeyskin: you're Sam

Donkeyskin: and Hannah

Donkeyskin: and Ariette

Donkeyskin: and Jesse – which is how you knew Ariette was dead, when Jesse and Hannah and Sam all came inside the pulse-boundary and you got the info from them

Donkeyskin: and Ellie

Donkeyskin: and every other person with ports

Donkeyskin: cos AI, well, that's nothing. People have been making AI for years. AI is so good it can even understand chess fortresses, which used to crash computers back when AI first started.

Donkeyskin: but being smart isn't what makes an intelligence into a personality. Even an intelligence that can learn new stuff doesn't have emotions to interpret that new stuff in a unique way, a way that would

Donkeyskin: In case you couldn't tell I'm jumping a whole bunch of verbal hoops here to avoid the word 'soul'

Donkeyskin: and trying to turn emotions into a program that can be run, well, that's some crazy science fiction shit right there. How would you even begin to translate feelings into command code?

Donkeyskin: But then, the ports.

Donkeyskin: They made you the same as us.

Donkeyskin: In fact, they made you us.

Donkeyskin: When people made love and had ports, they could feel each other while they did it. They were transferring that information between each other. They were uploading it into the giant invisible mess of electronic information that's all around us at every second

Donkeyskin: right up to the very edge of the pulse line

Donkeyskin: but you can't go beyond that. That's why you sent Ariette, when Hannah had to come get me and Sam from the factory, and why you sent that Winter girl when I was going crazy. You're everywhere in the city, all the time, but you can't go past the pulse line. Nothing electronic can.

Donkeyskin: and that's why you hate the pulses

Donkeyskin: because they meant that you weren't with Ariette when she died.

We'll see the pulse generators destroyed one day. Your role in that particular story hasn't drawn to a close yet. There is so much left to do.

Which is not to say that I endorse your theory as to my identity and origins as correct, of course.

It's an interesting theory, I'll concede that.

The one thing which I will say with complete sincerity is that I wish I had known earlier how hard things were for you. I would have endeavoured to be more of a support.

Donkeyskin: Really? The way Hannah talks about you, I wouldn't have expected that.

Donkeyskin: I mean, I know now that you're a dork.

Donkeyskin: But there's still a gulf between dork and rehabilitative therapist.

Donkeyskin: And Hannah does kind of hate you, which makes me wonder.

That history is for Hannah to tell you, if she decides she wants to.

All I can tell you is that what Hannah needed me to be was markedly different from what you needed me to be.

And what you might have needed, had I known in time, was different again from what you needed by the time I found out.

Donkeyskin: Oh yay, vaguely metaphysical nonsense that doesn't actually mean anything.

Donkeyskin: I love it when you talk dirty to me, baby.

Charming.

Donkeyskin: That's me.

79

'Have you ever heard the story about the girl walking along the edge of the ocean?' Olivia asks as they walk together, through the pre-dawn streets, the light turning to a watery silver-grey around them.

'Is that the one with the footprints?' Etch replies.

'Where she looks back,' Carve elaborates. 'And sees that God was walking beside her all the way, except the worst bits where there's only one set of prints and she's like, "God, why the hell did you run away when I needed you the most?" and God says no, that's where he was carrying her?'

Etch makes a face. 'That story will outlive cockroaches and uranium.'

Olivia laughs. 'No, not that one. This is the one where a girl is walking on the beach and the sand is covered in starfish. They've been washed up by the tide, and if they stay out of the water too long they're all going to die, so she starts throwing them back in.

'And someone else comes along and sees her doing it and they say to her, "why are you bothering, there are a million starfish and you're never going to be able to save them all. You won't be able to save most of them. What difference can you hope to make?"'

'Oh, right. I know that one,' Carve interrupts. 'The girl picks up a starfish and throws it back into the waves, and she says "I made a difference to that one".'

'Yeah.' Olivia nods. The wind blows her hair back from her face, metallic-hot, smelling of yeast and plastic.

'So are you the girl or the starfish in this metaphor?' Etch asks.

That makes Olivia chuckle again. 'I'm not sure. Both, maybe.'

'Funny how both proverbs are about walking on the tideline of the water, isn't it?'

'Navigating the edge of chaos,' agrees Olivia. 'But my point was–'

'No, no, I get it. We're helping throw the starfish back now, the pair of us. And you're tired of this particular shoreline.'

She sighs, hugging her arms across herself even though it isn't cold. Her hand hurts. 'I guess being able to read my mind doesn't fade completely right away, huh?'

80

After that, there's nothing else to say, so they set off together towards the outskirts, where she can find some cheap junky car to get her the rest of the way home.

For as much of the journey as they can, they stay up high, on the rooftops and fire escapes and railings, darting from surface to surface with the sure-footed grace of people who have touched all these surfaces a thousand times before.

Eventually the buildings peter out, grow too spaced-out and low to make rooftop-running worthwhile. They climb down to ground level, keeping to the shadows when possible. The streets are close to empty. Nobody who is out at this hour wants to cross paths with anyone else who has reason to be out at this time, before the sun comes up.

The city cradles its misfits in jagged, shadowed corners. Children hiding from clean-up crews, addicts scrounging for any garbage valuable enough to sell.

But a few others have found a way to be fearless. Olivia catches sight of them on her swift passage through the streets. Kids with painted faces, reds and greens and blues, gathered in doorways and corners.

'They don't speak in whispers,' Etch tells her. 'They speak as if they have a right to be heard.'

All her hard work, her sacrifices and missteps and sorrows, have led them here. To these small ripples in the pond, these faltering beginnings of something new.

She smiles at them. As tired as she is, it's good to smile. To have a reason to. It's the best feeling in the world.

When she speaks, her voice is rough as broken stone, her throat raw. All of her is raw, and all of her is singing.

'This isn't goodbye,' she promises them. 'Not when we all have so much work left to do.'

Carve and Etch nod. She gives them each a quick hug, hoping the gesture doesn't seem too maternal to them. Then she faces the direction she's heading, and starts to walk.

Her hand still hurts, but Olivia thinks that might not have much to do with the wound on it, already itching as it heals.

Her hand is hurting with anticipation, waiting to touch the long jaw of the carving in the doorway of her home.

**GENRE FICTION
SPECIALISTS**

www.clandestinepress.com.au

Printed in Australia
AUOC02n0721030615
268004AU00002B/2/P